Eye Candy

RUMOR
CENTRAL

Also by ReShonda Tate Billingsley

The Rumor Central Series

Rumor Central
You Don't Know Me Like That
Real As It Gets
Truth or Dare
Boy Trouble
Eye Candy

Published by Kensington Publishing Corp.

Eye Candy
RUMOR CENTRAL

RESHONDA TATE BILLINGSLEY

KENSINGTON PUBLISHING CORP.
www.kensingtonbooks.com

DAFINA BOOKS are published by

Kensington Publishing Corp.
119 West 40th Street
New York, NY 10018

All Kensington titles, imprints, and distributed lines are available at special quantity discounts for bulk purchases for sales promotion, premiums, fund-raising, and educational or institutional use.

Special book excerpts or customized printings can also be created to fit specific needs. For details, write or phone the office of the Kensington Special Sales Manager: Kensington Publishing Corp., 119 West 40th Street, New York, NY 10018. Attn. Special Sales Department. Phone: 1-800-221-2647.

Dafina and the Dafina logo Reg. U.S. Pat. & TM Off.
Sunburst logo Reg. U.S. Pat. & TM Off.

ISBN-13: 978-0-7582-8961-2
ISBN-10: 0-7582-8961-8
First Kensington Trade Paperback Printing: April 2015

eISBN-13: 978-0-7582-8962-9
eISBN-10: 0-7582-8962-6
First Kensington Electronic Edition: April 2015

10 9 8 7 6 5 4 3 2 1

Printed in the United States of America

Author's Note

I can't believe it's been six books since Maya Morgan came bursting onto the scene. I have had a blast writing about a character that's so unlike me. But that's the beauty of story-telling—letting your imagination run free.

I am so thankful to be doing something that I absolutely love doing. But I am even more grateful to you—the reader—for making everything I do worthwhile. So I end this *Rumor Central* series the same way I began. With a tremendous thank-you to the readers, young and not-so-young. To the teachers, parents, librarians, everyone who helped ignite a love of reading, thank you as well.

I must once again say thanks to my children, who were forever adding their ten cents on what Maya Morgan should be doing. My girls, Mya and Morgan . . . and my son, Myles . . . thank you for bearing with Mommy during the writing process.

I also have to shout out to my husband, and the rest of my wonderful family and friends who support and nurture my literary career. Gina Johnson, you know I never would've been able to finish this book without you! Sheretta Edwards and Yolanda Gore, thank you for making my life flow so much smoother. Maiya White and Crystal Green, thank you for sharing your creativity with me. I'm so happy to intro-duce the world to Nelly and Karrington, compliments of your imagination. Much thanks also to my hardworking agent, Sara Camilli, and my wonderful editor, Selena James, and the fantastic publicity team at Kensington Books!

Much love to my friends and sisters of the teen pen who also craft wonderful reads for young people, Stephanie Perry Moore, Ni-Ni Simone, Nikki Carter, Shelia Goss, Victoria

Christopher Murray, Jaqueline Thomas, and Earl Sewell. Make sure you check out their teen books as well!

Shoot me an email at reshondat@aol.com or follow me on Instagram at ReShonda Tate Billingsley and let me know what you think about *Rumor Central*. Can't wait to hear from you! If you've missed any of the previous five books, please check them out. You'll be glad you did!

Much love,
ReShonda

Chapter 1

I needed my own page in Webster's Dictionary. That's because, if you looked up the word *fabulous,* there I was. If you looked up *phenomenal,* you'd find my name. If you looked up *all that and then some,* yep, there I would be. Yeah, I know, nobody even uses dictionaries anymore, but you get what I'm sayin'.

I was Maya Morgan and I was off the chain.

I knew that sounded arrogant, but it was what it was.

I couldn't help who I was. And right about now, I was also the happiest girl on the planet. I was the most famous young talk show host in the country. My television show, *Rumor Central,* was still number one (as if there was anything else to be when it came to me). I was six weeks away from graduating high school. I had even managed to pull up my grades—even in that stupid calculus class, which yours truly was now rocking a C in.

And now, I had finally found love with the guy of my dreams. Yeah, I know at one time I'd thought that was Bryce, my lame ex-boyfriend, but Bryce was a *boy.* My new boo was a *man.* Actually, my new boo was Alvin Martin, one of my closest friends. Yes, he was twenty-one years old, but that was

only three years older than me, so I didn't know why anybody would trip. Besides, I couldn't deal with guys my age
because they were so immature. But our friendship was why
our relationship is going so well—we were friends first.

I dabbed some lip gloss on as I leaned into the ladies'-
room mirror and smiled. We were at an entertainment industry party and Alvin had once again held his own, which made
me love him that much more. Alvin and I were from two different worlds. He was a geek; I was a goddess. Alvin preferred
to stay in the background; I loved the limelight. Unlike my
other exes, Alvin let me have my shine with no complaint. I
couldn't say the same about Bryce, who went to school at
Miami High with me and couldn't stand all of the attention I
got, or my other ex, R & B singer J. Love, who was always
competing with my shine.

Alvin took a back seat and let me do me. Of course, I
couldn't forget the fact that he treated me so well, nor the
fact that even though you wouldn't know it by looking at
him, he was stupid rich. And now that I'd cleaned him up a
little bit, he wasn't half bad looking. I still hadn't been able to
get rid of those Coke-bottle glasses, but I was working on it.
Now, he looked less like Steve Urkel and more like Michael
B. Jordan, that cute guy from the movie *Fruitvale Station*.

I finally snapped out of my thoughts as I noticed the girl
washing her hands in the sink next to me was staring my way.

"Hi," I said, when I really wanted to ask her what her
problem was.

"Oh . . . my . . . God," she said, slowly, as if she'd been
trying to figure out who I was and it had just dawned on her.
"Are you Maya Morgan?"

I gave her a small nod and a smile, and she started jumping up and down.

"No way! No freakin' way!" She fumbled to get her
phone out of her purse. "Can I take a picture with you?" She

was already on the side of me before I could answer, so I just smiled as she snapped a selfie.

"OMG, I'm so putting this on Instagram," she said as she began tapping away on her phone.

"Nice to meet you," I said, dropping my lip gloss back in my purse and stepping around her to go into a stall.

She grabbed my arm and the look on my face must've made her think twice because she dropped my arm and said, "Sorry, I'm just so excited. I just want to say I love your show. I'm so glad they took you off *Miami Divas* and gave you your own show."

I smiled. I was happy about that, too. Before I ever made my first television appearance, I was already at the top of the food chain as the leader of Miami's "It Clique." In fact, that's why I'd been approached to do the reality show *Miami Divas* in the first place. But someone had a brain fart and put me with four other "rich chicks" as one magazine described us (even though, technically, Bali Fernandez, one of the "chicks" was a boy, he was more flamboyant than all of us put together). *Miami Divas* hadn't done as well as they'd wanted it to, so they'd canceled it and fired Bali and the other three costars—Evian Javid, Shay Turner, and my BFF, Sheridan Matthews. Of course, none of us were too thrilled about that. I'd quickly gotten over it though, when they'd announced I wouldn't be getting fired and instead would be getting my own show. Everybody had been so mad at me because we had all agreed that we were a team. I had honestly meant that— until the producers told me I was getting my own show. Then, all bets were off.

Evian, Bali, and Shay never got over it. And after a lot of drama, me and Sheridan (who was my BFF since like forever) had been able to squash things and go back to kickin' it.

That move to give me my own show had turned out to be the smartest thing the station could've done. I had become the go-to chick for all the latest celebrity gossip, dirt, and entertainment news. *Rumor Central* was now one of the top entertainment shows in the country.

". . . and I even DVR your show."

I hadn't even realized this girl was still rambling.

"Well, I really need to go," I said, pointing at the stall.

"Oh, sorry," the girl said, still excited. "I'll let you go. I can't believe I actually met Maya Morgan." She giggled as she made her way out the ladies' room.

I hated public restrooms but all of that Fiji Water (because I didn't do alcohol) I had been drinking was running straight through me. So, I stepped into the stall, thankful that this place at least kept their restrooms clean. I was handling my business when I heard the chatter of two girls as they walked in. I didn't pay them any attention until I heard one of them say my name.

"Girl, did you see that nerd boy Maya Morgan is with?" one of them said.

That made me stand on alert because of the nasty way it rolled off her tongue.

"I did. Everybody's talking about it," the other voice replied.

"I'm like, seriously, you dumped J. Love for *that*?"

J. Love was an R & B singer who had to be the hottest thing going right now. He was so fine, it was ridiculous. He had smooth chocolate skin, curly hair, and a body that was out of this world. He looked like a much finer version of Trey Songz. Yes, he was all that, but he could also be a jerk.

"I mean, really?" the first girl continued. "I could pull a guy better than that dork she's with."

"For real, what I wouldn't give to have J. Love. He is so fine!"

"Baby, fine ain't even the word. And from what I heard, he was really feeling her and she dumped him for *that*."

Their laughter mixed with running water as I stood deathly still, both angry and shocked.

One of the girls continued. "But did you see him on the dance floor, though? He doesn't have any rhythm."

I couldn't appreciate them talking about my guy like that, but as mad as I was, they were right. Alvin's attempt on the dance floor had been embarrassing, to say the least. I couldn't bring myself to come out of the stall.

"All I know is I *used* to envy Maya Morgan, but, baby, if that's the best she can do, I think I'll stay me!"

Their laughter drifted off as they walked out of the restroom.

I didn't move for a few minutes. Then, finally, I pushed open the door, and made my way out of the stall. I stared at my reflection in the European-tiled mirror. Had I really been reduced to that chick who got talked about in the bathroom?

Were people really talking about my man?

Finally, I took a deep breath and told myself it wasn't about what they wanted. It wasn't about what anyone wanted. I was feeling Alvin and he was feeling me. And that's all that mattered—right?

I shook myself out of my trance, washed my hands, and headed back out. I had just walked back to the VIP area when I saw Alvin standing outside of the roped area.

"Hey, babe, what's up?" I asked, wondering why he was out here and not inside the VIP area at our private table.

"I came to check on you because you were gone so long and now they won't let me back in."

"What do you mean, they won't let you in?" I didn't wait for a reply as I stomped back over to the bouncer standing at the door to the VIP room.

"Excuse me. My boyfriend said you won't let him in. He has a VIP bracelet," I said, trying not to get an attitude as I jabbed my finger in Alvin's direction.

The burly bald-headed bouncer looked at me and then

looked at Alvin. "Oh, dude, my bad. I thought you stole that or something." He stepped aside and then chuckled to his friend standing on the side of him. "I didn't know they were letting bustas in the VIP now."

I rolled my eyes as I stomped past them. Alvin was right on my heels. This was the second time tonight someone had disrespected my man and I was getting fed up. I had tried my best not to be *that* chick. But these people were definitely trying to push me.

Chapter 2

I used to think that Alvin's nerdy dancing looked cute. But right about now I'd give anything if he'd just stop. Maybe it was because of what those girls in the bathroom had said. Maybe it was because of the way people were standing around snickering. And I didn't like that Alvin didn't seem bothered by any of it, including not being able to get back into the VIP area. Had it been me, I would've gone clean off on the bouncer. But Alvin acted like it was no big deal.

He finally stopped dancing when he noticed me barely moving. "What's wrong, babe?" he asked.

I just stared at him. If there was one thing I would change about Alvin, it would be his nonchalant attitude. He wasn't weak. He just rarely got upset—even when he had every right to. Yeah, I'd change that. And his style. And his nerdy ways. Oh yeah, and those glasses. They would definitely be gone. Other than that, I liked him just as he was. But I was definitely going to have to have a talk with him about this.

I'd first met Alvin when a friend of my other BFF, Kennedi, put me in touch with him so he could help me figure out who was hacking into my email account. Alvin was some kind of computer whiz (he even made a lot of money off one of his computer inventions).

Alvin liked me from jump, but he was a nerd with a capital N. He was a rich nerd, but he was a nerd nonetheless, so I wouldn't give him the time of day like that. But Alvin had a great sense of humor and a knack for making me laugh, and eventually, I fell in love with him.

"You're not still mad about that bouncer, are you?" Alvin asked as if he were reading my mind.

"And I can't believe you're not," I replied.

He shrugged. "Life is too short to be walking around mad. The bouncer didn't know who I was. You cleared it up; it's over." He began doing that stupid wiggle dance again to the sound of DJ Snake and Lil Jon's "Turn Down for What."

"Whatever, Alvin." I was about to turn and go back to my seat.

Alvin actually stopped dancing, took my hand, and studied me. "You're for-real mad? Come on, babe. Just relax and enjoy yourself." He started dancing harder. He almost reminded me of Carlton off of those *Fresh Prince of Bel-Air* reruns.

I couldn't help it. I actually giggled. "Okay. I'll get over it if you promise to just stop dancing."

"What?" he said, doing a quick spin around. "You don't think I could try out for *America's Got Talent*?"

"Um, that would be no," I said, laughing.

"Yo, I say go for it. I bet you could win."

We stopped and both of us turned to see my ex, J. Love, standing there, a big grin on his face. I wanted to die. I'd purposely asked the event organizer if J. Love was going to be here and he'd said no. I'd even gone as far as texting J. Love to find out if he was in town, and when he hadn't responded, I'd assumed that he wasn't.

"What's up, Maya?" J. said with a huge smile. He and I

had been a serious item for a few months. Until someone had leaked some info about him to the *National Enquirer* and he'd just naturally assumed it was me. It had turned out to be this girl who was obsessed and stalking me, but because of the whole way J. had handled the situation, I had been too through.

"Hey J.," I said. J. Love put Alvin to shame in the looks department. There was a reason he was one of the top singers in the country right now.

"You're looking good," J. said, licking his lips as if I were a pork chop.

Alvin stepped right in front of me, I guess guarding his territory.

"What's up, my man? Andrew right?" J. Love asked, directing his huge, charming smile in Alvin's direction.

"Naw, dude, it's Alvin," Alvin said, suddenly getting a cockiness that I actually liked. "But you know that, right?"

"Alvin, Alvin, that's right," J. Love said, snapping his fingers. "You're like a computer geek."

"I prefer computer guru, but yeah, that would be me."

If J. Love was trying to insult Alvin, he definitely wasn't doing a good job because Alvin didn't seem fazed.

"Yo, ma," J. Love said, looking around Alvin so that our eyes could meet, "you enjoying the party?"

Once again, Alvin stepped in front of me to block J.'s view. "Her name is Maya, not ma, but I'm sure you know that, too."

J. licked his lips again. "Oh, I know that. I know that very well."

I stepped up to defuse any situation. I liked J. Love, I really did, and the public had liked us together. But even though I had forgiven him from tripping with me about the *Enquirer* story, my heart wasn't with him. I felt like we had been more for show than anything else. He loved having Maya Morgan on his arm, but he didn't *love* Maya Morgan. Not like Alvin did anyway.

"Don't you have a concert somewhere you need to be performing?" I asked.

"That's tomorrow in Tampa. Want me to fly you up?"

"Oh, that would be cool," Alvin said with a big grin. "What time should we be ready to go?"

I couldn't help but smile.

J. Love actually laughed, too. "I like him," J. said to me. "He's quick witted."

Alvin took my hand.

"And a little possessive," J. Love added.

"Bye, J.," I said, dismissing him.

But before I could turn and walk away, someone yelled, "Maya, J.! This way!" I was about to go off because the paparazzi wasn't supposed to be able to get into the VIP area. But then I noticed it was actually the photographer assigned by the party promoters.

"Yo, can I get a closer shot of you two?" he asked, motioning between me and J. Love.

"Um, yeah, that's probably not a good idea." I held up my hand, which was still intertwined with Alvin's.

"Oh, come on now," the photographer replied.

"Yeah, come on now," J. Love repeated. "I mean, I'm sure your man won't mind. Will you, *Alvin*?" he said, stressing his name to make sure he got it right.

Alvin eased in front of me just a bit.

"Dude, it's just a photo," the photographer said, staring at Alvin like he didn't understand the problem.

Alvin looked at me. I didn't know what I was supposed to do, but all eyes were on me, so I just shrugged. "He's right. It's just a stupid picture."

Alvin gave me a look like that really wasn't the answer that he was looking for, but he let my hand go and stepped to the side. I moved closer to J. Love and the photographer immediately began taking pictures of me with J. Love. The flash of the bulbs brought more photographers and before we knew it, there were about five or six photographers snapping away and tossing questions our way. I guess once one of them got in, the rest jumped the rope as well.

I wanted to stop and ask why they were letting the photographers in VIP, but the last thing I wanted to do was get on their bad side. But when one of them said, "Are you guys back together?" I knew it was time to shut it down.

"Oh my God, you guys make such a cute couple!" someone else added.

"Sorry, folks, I'm not with J. Love." I stepped away from him and draped my arm through Alvin's. "This is my man."

In what seemed like a scene out of a movie, the whole place went quiet. Then there were a few snickers, then all-out laughter.

Then, someone in the back of the room yelled, "Are you freaking kidding me?"

Finally, a reporter that I actually *did* like said, "What's his name?"

"Alvin Martin," I said. "He's the sweetest guy you will ever meet." That made Alvin finally smile. "Here, why don't you guys get a few shots of us?" I asked, pulling Alvin toward me. One lone camera began flashing as the other photographers actually started putting their cameras up and walking away. I don't think I've ever been so embarrassed in all my life.

And once again, my boyfriend didn't seem fazed as he grinned for the one photographer.

Chapter 3

I loved hanging with my girls, especially now that Sheridan and Kennedi—my two BFFs—were getting along good. Now, since Kennedi had moved back to Miami from Orlando and was finishing up her senior year at school with us, we were three BFFs.

For the longest time though, the two of them couldn't stand each other. Even though I'd known both of them since I was little, they just couldn't get along. Sheridan—the daughter of mega pop star and actress Glenda Matthews—was a brainiac who pretty much did what she wanted, when she wanted, since her mother stayed on the road all the time. Sheridan's aunts lived with her and were supposed to be keeping an eye on her, but they were usually too busy traveling themselves—off Ms. Glenda's money—to be bothered.

Kennedi was the laid-back one. Or she used to be. She'd just come off some major drama with her ex-boyfriend and was currently in therapy to get her temper under control, so she'd been trying to take everything in stride lately.

I think each of them used to be jealous of my friendship with the other, which is why they were always going at it. But thankfully, over the past few months, we all had gotten really close. And I loved it.

Today, we were chillin' at Orange Leaf Yogurt, enjoying a beautiful Saturday afternoon and people watching. After making a lot of small talk, Sheridan said, "So I heard about J. Love at the club the other night. Why didn't you tell me?"

I shrugged. "What was there to tell?" I replied. "J. Love was just being his usual arrogant self."

"Mmm-hmm," Kennedi said, smiling. "He was all up in that magazine talking about how much he loves you."

I shook my head. The *Miami Hot Gossip* magazine had just come out yesterday and I prayed that Alvin hadn't seen it. Not that I had done anything wrong, but it was just straight disrespectful. Not only had they made Alvin look like some kind of nerdy creep, but every picture they had used had Alvin lurking in the background. It looked like J. Love and I were the couple, and not me and Alvin.

"So what are you going to do?" Kennedi asked.

"What do you mean, what am I going to do?" I replied. "I'm going to do what I've been doing." I slid a spoonful of the low-fat yogurt into my mouth.

Both of them looked at me like I was crazy.

I studied them for a minute. "Are you all serious? I thought you both liked Alvin."

"Oh, we do. It's just that everybody else *loves* J. Love," Sheridan said, snickering.

"Since when do I care what everyone else thinks?" I snapped.

"Um, since always," Kennedi replied. They started giggling like something was really funny.

I waved my spoon in their direction. "That's not the point. The point is Alvin is my boyfriend. End of story." I guess the tone of my voice let them know that I was getting an attitude because they threw up their hands like they were done talking about it. Of course, that didn't last long because after five minutes of talking about some drama from school, we were right back on Alvin.

"So, you're going to take Alvin to the Icon Awards?" Sheridan asked, referring to the biggest award show outside of the Oscars. It was being held in Miami in a couple of weeks.

"Why wouldn't I?" I asked.

"You're really going to have him on the red carpet?" Kennedi asked. She was acting like I was taking Flavor Flav or something.

"And again, why wouldn't I?"

Both of them shrugged and that made me do a double take. I dropped my spoon back into my bowl as I glared at both of them. "If you have something to say, say it."

They exchanged glances and, finally, it was Kennedi who spoke first.

"Look, you know we like Alvin. We really do. He's a cool guy, but he makes your stock go down," she said.

"That's jacked up," I replied, stunned not only that my friends actually felt like this, but that they were sitting here talking about my boyfriend.

"It is jacked up," Sheridan added. "But it is what it is."

They exchanged glances again, and then Kennedi said, "Are you going to tell her or not?"

Sheridan gave her a "shut up" look and now I found myself getting mad.

"Okay, you two better get to talking and tell me what's going on." When nobody answered, I slammed my hand on the table and said, "Now!"

They jumped a little bit and then Sheridan said, "Look, Savannah Vanderpool told me word from the award folks is that they don't want you on the red carpet unless you're with J. Love."

"What?" I said, shocked. Since when do they get to dictate who someone brings on the red carpet?

"Savannah Vanderpool knows someone who knows someone, who works with the event coordinator," Sheridan continued. "Apparently, they like the whole Maya—J. Love thing. And when they extended the invitation for you to walk the red carpet, they just assumed you'd be walking with J. Love."

"Why would they assume that?" I asked.

Both of them shrugged.

"Apparently, they saw the *Miami Hot Gossip* pics, so they had Savannah call me this morning to get the scoop," Sheridan said.

I couldn't believe what I was hearing. "So, I'll walk by my dang self, if it's that big of a deal."

"I think they want you with J.," Sheridan said, giving me a *don't kill the messenger* look.

"Well, I don't care what they want," I said. I was in a foul mood now. I was sick and tired of everyone trying to put me with J. Love. Been there, done that, had the T-shirt to prove it didn't work.

"Look, it's probably no biggie. I'm sure they'll be happy with you and your man on the red carpet," Kennedi tossed in.

The way Sheridan averted her eyes and looked down, I definitely knew that wouldn't be the case.

All I wanted was to live my fabulous life and love my wonderful boyfriend. Why in the world did everything have to be so difficult?

Chapter 4

Despite my hectic world, I enjoyed this time most of all. Just chilling with Alvin, watching movies. It was a perfect way to finish a Saturday night. We'd just finished watching *Scary Movie 5* and we'd laughed like it was the funniest thing ever, even though it was corny as all get out. But just hanging around Alvin was so relaxing, and it made me say screw all that mess everyone else was talking, this was where my happiness was.

"So you want to watch another one?" Alvin said, as he popped the disc out of the Blu-ray player.

"No, I'm not going to be able to stay much longer. My mom will call out the SWAT team looking for me soon," I replied. My parents stayed super busy—my dad running the Morgan chain of hotels, and my mom spending the money my dad made from the Morgan chain of hotels. But they still tried to keep track of my whereabouts and would seriously get to tripping if I didn't come home at a decent hour.

Alvin placed the disc back in its case, and I grabbed the remote and flipped it to MTV.

"So finish telling me, when is the new design going to come out?" I asked.

Alvin was working on yet another patent. This time, it was something that would revolutionize the Internet experience, and he was super excited.

"Soon. My attorney is working out some last-minute legal stuff," he said. He was just about to say something else when I noticed his eyes zoom in on the TV.

I turned to see what he was looking at. One of the MTV VJs was interviewing J. Love. I groaned and reached for the remote to change the channel.

"No," Alvin said, putting his hand over mine to stop me. "Let's see what your boy is talking about today." He took the remote from me and turned the volume up just as the VJ said, "So you're really feeling her?"

My eyebrow rose. Feeling her? J. Love was so disrespectful. Flirting with me yesterday and raving about some other girl today.

"Oh, I'm definitely feeling her," he told the female VJ. "In fact, I'm in love with her and she's in love with me, too. She's just in denial right now."

"That is so sweet. You're a man after my own heart," the VJ said, before turning back to talk to the camera. "Well, you heard it here, ladies and gentlemen. I asked J. Love about the women in his life and he said there's only one woman he wants, so Maya Morgan, girl, you better get this man."

My mouth fell open and Alvin lost his smile. Who in their right mind went on national TV and proclaimed his love for a woman who wasn't his? I stared at the TV, dumbstruck.

"Yeah, you know my boys might not be feeling what I'm doing," J. Love continued, all but taking the mic back from the VJ, "but Maya is my soul mate. I feel it right here." He tapped his chest, and the VJ swooned.

"Oh my God! You're, like, so perfect!" she said.

I reached for the remote, grabbed it out of Alvin's hand, then snapped the TV off.

"He's so perfect, huh?" Alvin said, his nose turned up in disgust.

"Come on, Alvin. Really?"

"Whatever, Maya." He stomped out of the living room. Why in the world was he mad at me? I hadn't done anything.

"Seriously, you're going to be mad at me because of something J. Love did?" I asked, following him.

He spun around, a serious expression on his face. "Maya, you need to shut him down."

"You don't think I tried that?" I told Alvin. "Every time he calls and texts, I shut him down."

Alvin cocked his head in shock. "So he's still calling and texting?"

I wanted to kick myself in the mouth. "I mean, sometimes he calls . . . you know, just to check on me."

"Oh, and you didn't think that was something I needed to know?"

"Really, Alvin? We're going to seriously fight over my ex?"

"Yeah, when your ex is all over TV talking about he's in love with you."

At that moment, I wished I could get the nerdy Alvin back because this one that was trying to jump bad was actually not a good look.

"Look, Alvin," I said. "I don't want J. Love. I want you. I'm here with you. I can't control what he does."

"Whatever, Maya." He actually waved me off like he was dismissing me or something.

"I just don't believe this," I said, standing and grabbing my purse. "When you get out of your funky attitude, call me. I'll be at home."

I stomped toward the front door. And then I was shocked when he actually let me walk out the door without trying to stop me.

Chapter 5

I couldn't believe I'd wasted twenty minutes lost in my thoughts. Alvin had called me before I went to bed last night. He'd apologized for getting jealous and we'd made up. But I couldn't get J. Love out of my mind. Several blogs had picked up his MTV interview and now it was all over the Internet. Why was he going so hard to get me back?

Even my cousin Travis had weighed in. Since we were only a few months apart, Travis and I were extremely close. He'd lived with us for a while a few months ago, but he'd moved back home to Brooklyn, New York, because his mom was really sick. We'd been keeping in touch via text and Instagram and he'd just texted me, Do u getting back w JL? Lol.

I quickly typed back. No. Hes so out of order. Call u later.

I wished I had time to call him then, but it was like I was always too busy and running here and there.

No sooner had that thought crossed my mind than my assistant, Yolanda, poked her head in my office door.

"Excuse me," Yolanda said. The look on her face told me her news wasn't going to be good. Her lips were puckered up, like she was in the middle of a disgusting kiss, and she wouldn't look me in the face.

"Um, please tell me you're just tired, constipated, or something," I said, dropping my cell phone back into my purse.

Yolanda didn't say a word as she handed me a letter-sized envelope. "Your tickets to the Icon Awards are in there."

"And I'm sitting in a prime spot, right?" I said, taking the envelope. No way was I going to make my debut at the Icon Awards sitting in a jacked-up seat.

"Um, I don't know exactly where the seats are, but, um . . ." She shifted nervously.

"But what? Spit it out," I said, tearing the envelope open.

"I *do* know that they're in the balcony area," she said, taking a step back as if I were going to lash out at her.

"Balcony!" I screamed as I jumped up from my chair. "Are you freaking kidding me?" I pulled the tickets from the envelope and almost passed out when I saw *balcony* printed on them.

"I don't—"

I cut her off. "Oh, I don't think so! Maya Morgan doesn't do balconies! You need to get on the phone right now!" I yelled.

"Th-that's actually what I've been doing for the last thirty minutes," she stammered.

I could tell that she was nervous as all get out, but she had reason to be because I wouldn't even go to the awards ceremony, before I sat in somebody's balcony.

Yolanda continued. "I talked to the planning producer and they said that the seating was specifically done—"

I interrupted her again. "Well, who is *they*? *They* obviously don't know who I am. You need to talk to a supervisor or something."

"I did, because I knew you weren't going to be happy."

"You're doggone right I'm not happy!" I screamed, slamming the envelope down on my desk. "I'm Maya Morgan and they want to put *me* in the balcony?"

"The booking producer said they could find you *one* seat up front."

"*One* seat?" I said, raising an eyebrow. Now I knew what this was all about. If I leave Alvin at home, I can get a decent seat. If I want to bring my man I have to sit in the balcony? Part of me wanted to go off and tell all of them what they could do for me. But I wasn't going to go out like that.

"Fine, if that's how they want to play the game, that's how we'll play it." I grabbed my earpiece, checked myself in the mirror, then headed back to the studio. We were doing a story today on pop star Rickey Gold's spiral downhill. All that money must've been going to his head because he was straight losing it. Today we had an interview with some stripper whom he'd allegedly assaulted so I needed to be focused.

"Do you want me to keep trying?" Yolanda asked.

"You know what?" I told her right before I left out of my office. "Don't worry about it. If they think they can break Maya Morgan, they need to think again."

I made my way onto the set and tried to get my head together.

"Stand by, Maya," the director, Manny, said, giving me my cue as the *Rumor Central* theme music started playing. "And five, four, three, two . . ." He pointed at me and I began talking.

"What's up, everyone? It's your girl, Maya Morgan, and have we got the scoop for you." I delivered my signature intro with my signature flare, then went on to give the scoop on Rickey Gold. Even though the show was good, my heart wasn't in it and I couldn't wait for this show to wrap up.

I had built up my show by breaking all the hot celeb stories. I'd caught a lot of flak because when I'd started, the producers had given me the whole "you need to bring the dirt or get canceled" speech. So I'd sold out a lot of my celeb friends and it had created major drama. But the more popular the show got, the more power I got, so I had told them that

I'd bring dirt, but not from my own backyard. The ratings were down a little, but I was still at the top of my game.

As soon as I got the all clear, I headed to my office. I didn't even sit down at my desk. I grabbed my keys and headed out to my car. During the commercials, I found myself thinking about the balcony and my blood began to boil all over again. My hands were even shaking as I punched in Alvin's name on my cell phone.

"Hey, babe," he said, answering on the first ring. "Good show!"

"Thanks."

"What's wrong?" he asked.

"I'm having a bad day."

"What happened?"

"I just had some drama with the Icon Awards show," I moaned.

"Oh, I thought something was *really* wrong." He laughed.

I rolled my eyes. If there was one thing that I didn't like about Alvin, it was how, even though he was supportive of what I did, he would, from time to time, make these little comments like he thought my world was frivolous. I was about to say something when I saw a text come in. I pulled my phone away from my ear and glanced at the screen. The message was from J. Love.

Heard about ur ticket drama.

Then another one:

Let me know if u need me to pull some strings. I got u.

And another one:

I'm on the 2nd row.

I wanted to scream.

"Hello?" Alvin said, turning my attention back to the phone.

"Sorry, I was just distracted."

"I was trying to say—"

"Hey, um, can I call you back?" I asked, cutting him off. I

didn't want to be rude, but I needed to talk to someone who understood what I was going through, and right about now that definitely wasn't my boyfriend.

"Oh." He paused. "Okay."

"Thanks. Call you back in a bit." I hung up and scrolled through my phone until I got to J.'s number. He answered on the first ring, like he had been waiting on my call.

"Hey, beautiful," he said.

"How do you know I have ticket drama?" I demanded to know.

I could feel him smiling through the phone. "Now, Maya, you know I know people who know people." He laughed at my silence. "Seriously, I don't have a date. Someone suggested I take you, and then someone else told me they heard you would be sitting in the balcony with Alfred."

Why was anyone telling him my business? I shook my head. Sometimes I hated this entertainment business. "You know his name is Alvin," I said.

"Whatever. I'm just saying, if you want to leave ol' dude at home, you know you can roll with me," J. Love said. "Prime seats, baby."

I can't believe it, but I actually thought about it for a moment. But then I came to my senses and said, "Nah, I'm good. Don't worry about me." I wasn't going to give J. Love the benefit of seeing me upset. I had planned to vent to him, but his cocky attitude made me change my mind.

"Okay," J. Love replied. "Just know I got you if you change your mind."

"Thanks, but my boyfriend has got me. So I'm straight," I responded.

He laughed like he knew better. "If you say so."

"I say so."

"A'ight, Maya Morgan, I'll talk to you soon."

"Bye," I said, hanging up the phone, angrier than I had been before I'd dialed his number.

Chapter 6

The halls of WSVV, the station that aired *Rumor Central,* were adorned with pictures of me with celebrities. With all these photos lined up along the wall, a person would've thought that I'd been doing this show for years.

I stopped at the photo of me and J. Love, which we'd taken the first time I'd interviewed him. I made a memo to myself to tell maintenance to take that picture down. But right now, I was on a mission.

I rounded the corner to my boss, Tamara's office. Before she got all crazy on me about ratings, back when I interned with her before we actually started *Miami Divas*, Tamara and I were really cool. Even though we weren't as close as we used to be, I felt like I could talk to her about anything, and I needed her professional and girlfriend opinion.

"Hey, Tamara, you got a minute?" I said, lightly tapping on her door. Her new secretary, Kelley, had already gone for the day, but I knew I'd find Tamara back here working away. It's no wonder she didn't have a boyfriend. She practically lived at this station.

"Yeah, come on in." Tamara waved me in. For it to be

seven o'clock in the evening, she still looked fly. She had on a silk V-neck blouse that looked like it was from the new Rachel Roy collection and a pencil skirt that flattered her size-six frame. She was sitting behind her desk, hands poised on her computer's keyboard. "Let me just send this email." She paused like she was thinking. "This new marketing campaign is driving me crazy. It's like nobody can make a decision about anything." She pounded the keyboard for a few minutes and then hit the ENTER button before letting out a long sigh. "Done," she said, then leaned back in her chair. "Now what's up?"

"Well . . ." I took a seat in one of the plush wingback chairs in front of her desk. "I needed to ask your opinion. You're still single, right?"

"Happily single." She smiled. "I've had my share of boyfriends, but boyfriends come with drama. They want your time and I don't have time." She narrowed her eyes at me. "And I understand you're all in love with this guy Alvin, but your star is shining brightly. The last thing you need is to be caught up in a serious relationship. Especially . . ." She caught herself and stopped talking.

"Especially what?" I asked.

"Nothing, Maya." She waved her hand, as if that would make her words go away.

"No, go ahead and say it," I said. "Are you thinking what everyone else is thinking? Especially with someone like Alvin? Is that what you were going to say?"

Tamara had met Alvin several times since he came up to the station quite a bit. She had always acted like she liked him. But now, I wasn't so sure.

Tamara gave me a sympathetic smile. "Well, if you want me to be honest, yeah. From what I know of the guy, he's as sweet as they come, but truthfully that's not what you need in your life right now. I don't expect you to be like me and be single forever. Maybe you *are* cut out for the whole mother-hood and marriage thing—I'm not. But I'm saying, right now, you don't need to be serious with anyone."

"But I love him," I protested. I had come to that realiza-tion about two months ago. After watching both Sheridan and Kennedi go through their share of boy troubles, I'd real-ized that a lot of times, we girls chase after what we think is the glittery prize, while the real prize is right under our noses all along. Alvin was my prize.

"Yeah, I get it. You love Alvin. And you loved Bryce, and you loved J. Love," Tamara reminded me.

"I didn't love J. Love," I responded defensively.

"Well, if anyone, that's the one you should've been lov-ing."

"What's that supposed to mean?" I said.

She leaned back in her leather chair. "Maya, I'm just going to shoot straight with you because that's the only way I do it. You are at the top of your game, and in this business, the way you stay at the top of your game is by staying relevant and keeping some eye candy on your arm."

"And I guess Alvin isn't eye candy?"

That actually made her laugh. "Girl, Alvin isn't even a peppermint."

I felt myself tearing up—and that wasn't easy because I usually didn't sweat what anyone thought. But Alvin was my heart and I hated that everybody was tearing him down.

"But he's sweet to me and he's good to me," I protested.

"And when you're forty-five and out of the business, that will be wonderful. That's exactly what you'll need. But for now, you need someone that will help continue to make your stock go up."

I guess she could tell that I was getting a little agitated be-cause her tone softened and she leaned back over her desk.

"You know, Maya, I'm not going to tell you who to love, but you asked my opinion and I gave it to you. Professionally,

Alvin is bad business for a girl like you, a girl who everyone wants to be like. Pretty soon you'll fall by the wayside as one of those non-factors," she said matter-of-factly.

"I'm going to always be a factor," I said defiantly.

She let out a heavy sigh. "Look at Beyoncé and Jay Z. Why do you think they're on top of the world?"

"Um, because they're Beyoncé and Jay-Z."

"True, and separately they're already the bomb, but together they're a mega explosion. That's you and J. Love. Kim and Kanye. Justin and Selena. Same thing."

"Justin and Selena broke up," I said.

She rolled her eyes. "My point is, people envy Maya Morgan. They want her life. Her clothes, her style, her fortune, her fame. And her man. As long as they admire you, you stay at the top of the game. Besides, it's hard in this business having a relationship with someone that's outside the business."

"Oh no, Alvin's not like that at all. He's completely cool." *For the most part*, I wanted to add, but I didn't say anything.

"Yeah, he is cool now, but there will come a point when you're doing your thing and it's going to become a problem," she replied.

"Okay," I said, tired of hearing her put down my guy. She hadn't made me feel better. Only worse. I stood. "I appreciate your input, Tamara."

Tamara smiled. "No, you don't, but one day you will." She winked.

"Okay, fine. I'm gonna head on out." I moved toward the door.

"Maya, at your age, it's nothing wrong with going for the one that can get you where you need to go. There's plenty of time for love later on," she called out as I headed out the door.

"Okay, thanks again." I walked out of the office before she continued her lecture. I don't know what I'd expected Tamara to say. I should've expected her to say exactly what she had.

For her, this wasn't about *who* was best for me, this was about *what* was best for my career. But why couldn't I have love *and* fame?

Even as I thought about that question, I knew me and I knew as much as I cared for Alvin, if I was truthful with myself, I knew that I wasn't ready to watch my career go down the toilet. And if that meant hiding my boyfriend and hanging out with J. Love, I might seriously have to consider doing that.

Chapter 7

I must have really been in love. That was the only thing that could explain why I was hesitating to do what I was about to do. The old Maya Morgan wouldn't have thought twice; it would've been all about me. But Alvin was a good guy and I really hated hurting him.

I didn't know what else to do though. I'd thought long and hard about this and I was going to have to take J. Love up on his offer. I simply could not sit in the balcony. My career was on the line and I really didn't want to jeopardize it. Plus, I didn't need any distractions at the Icon Awards. And I was really tired of having to defend my relationship.

I took a deep breath and rang the doorbell to Alvin's house. I'd practiced my speech all the way over here and I knew that, as hard as it was, I was going to have to uninvite him to the awards show.

"Hi, Mrs. Martin," I said to his mother, who was making a rare appearance to open the door. Usually, she stayed in her room. She was sickly, which was why she lived with Alvin. When I'd first met him, I had been turned off because I'd thought he was some nerd living at home. But, it turned out, he'd bought his childhood home, which his mother had lost several years prior, then moved her back in with him.

"Hey, sweetie," she said. I felt so bad for her. She was battling lupus, and most of the time, the disease looked as if it was winning. Today, she had on a blue housecoat, and her eyes looked dark and sunken. Her frail frame and her stringy hair made her look twenty years older than she actually was.

"Is Alvin here?" I asked.

Despite looking sickly, she had a big grin on her face. "He is," she said, stepping aside and motioning for me to come in. "He asked me to tell you to come on in and have a seat."

I walked into their living room and sat on the edge of the sofa.

"Can I get you anything?" she asked.

I shook my head. "No, ma'am. I'm good."

She had a mischievous look on her face and I didn't know what to make of it. The woman had probably said ten words to me in the entire time that I'd known her, so I didn't know what the look on her face was about.

"Just wait right there," she said.

"Okay. But do you know how long Alvin is going to be?" I asked. It was unlike Alvin to keep me waiting.

"Just a few minutes," she said, a little too loud.

I tried not to look at her crazy as she said, "Let me turn on the television for you."

"Oh, I'm good," I said.

"No, no, no. I have to turn the TV on," she firmly said.

"Okay, fine," I replied.

She smiled as she went to turn the TV on. She set the remote on top of the TV, then turned to me. "I'm going to leave you here to watch TV."

"Okay." I don't know why she was acting so strange. But I didn't feel like trying to figure it out either. So I just sat back and waited. After a few seconds, I heard music from the television. Then, a voice.

"Once upon a time, a friend called and asked if I could help out a friend of a friend." Alvin walked into the view on the screen. I frowned in confusion. Why had he taped a video? "Because I get those kind of calls all the time, I wasn't too thrilled about once again having to provide my services to someone free of charge," he continued. "Then, that friend of a friend showed up at my door. From the moment I saw her, I knew. I knew that she was special. I knew that, one day, she would be mine. But I also knew that she was way out of my league. So I could only dream. I dreamed that one day she would see in me, what I see in her. I dreamed that one day she would see that none of that celebrity life mattered. That the only thing that mattered was having someone in her life that really and truly loved her. That guy is me." The camera zoomed in closer as Alvin continued. Even though I had been trying to figure out what was going on, my heart was swelling.

"Maya, I don't even know if you remember that exactly one year ago today is when we first met. And on this, our anniversary, I want to say, I want to continue to be your best friend, your partner, and when you're ready, your lover. I will spend every day trying to make you happy."

By the time the video finished playing, I was in tears. Alvin had been so understanding about everything. Even though he was trippin' a little bit about J. Love lately, he put up with a lot and genuinely wanted me to be happy. Not to mention how understanding he'd been that I wanted to save myself (yeah, I know, a rarity). Not that I was waiting for marriage, but I was waiting for when the time was right.

"Maya, thank you for being in my life," Alvin said as the music came back up. Just then, Alvin appeared in the doorway with a bouquet of roses. "I hope those are happy tears," he said.

I stood up and hugged him. "They are. That was so sweet."

He handed me the flowers. "I know you can afford to buy anything I would've bought you, and I wanted to give you something from the heart. So, that's why I made this video. And these flowers are handpicked from my mother's rose garden." I took the bouquet and sniffed it.

"Maya, you are my best friend, and while I'm in no rush to do anything, I just want to make you happy. Whatever that may mean," Alvin added.

I hugged him tightly. Then tossed the speech I had been practicing from my mind. Forget what everyone else said. Alvin was the love of my life, and I would proudly have him on my arm at the Icon Awards—even if that meant we'd be sitting in the balcony.

Chapter 8

I didn't care what anyone said tonight, I was going to have a good time. That was the mantra I had been repeating to myself all evening long as I got dressed in my Christian Dior metallic silver gown. Alvin had proven he was worthy of being on my arm, and I needed to hold my head high as he escorted me to the awards show.

I knew that the evening was off to a great start when Alvin showed up to pick me up wearing an Armani tux. I had dropped several hints and then come right out and told him that he needed to bring his A game for this event. He'd blown me off and told me don't worry about it, he had it. Then, he'd refused my request to send me pictures of his tux. I'd gotten him sized and I had a backup tux upstairs—one of my dad's expensive ones that he'd never miss. I'd already had the waist taken in since Alvin was a little bit smaller than my dad. No way was I going to have this night ruined because Alvin was dressed like a nerd. I'd seen him dress up before, but I needed a backup plan just in case. Luckily, I didn't need it because Alvin was on it.

"You look nice," I said, giving him a once-over as he

stood in the foyer of our house. "Except . . ." I stepped toward him and removed his Coke-bottle glasses. "There."

"But I can't see!" I knew he was joking. Stuff was a little blurry, he'd told me before, but he could still see.

"I'll guide you," I said anyway. "But you look perfect now."

"He sure does." My mom approached us, smiling.

"Hello, Mrs. Morgan," Alvin said, politely.

"How are you, sweetheart?" she said, leaning in and giving him an air kiss.

My mom totally liked Alvin. I do think there was a part of her that felt like everyone else and wished he had a little more swag, but he was so polite and she loved the way he treated me, so she gave him a pass.

"Thank you very much," he replied.

"Is that Armani?" my mother asked, fingering his collar. As a devout shopaholic, she knew designers like she knew her own name. Guess that's where I got it from.

Alvin nodded. "Yes, ma'am. Custom."

My mom nodded her approval as she looked at me. "I like. I like."

We made some more small talk before Alvin finally said, "Are you ready to go?"

"Don't I look ready?" I asked, doing a slow twirl.

"That you do," he replied. "That you do."

We said our good-byes and made our way out to his fire-red Corvette. Twenty minutes later, we were pulling up to the American Airlines Arena. This was the first time the awards were being held somewhere other than L.A. and I needed to make sure I made a big splash. As soon as our limo pulled up to the red carpet, the show liaison met us at the door.

Alvin got out first, and the woman all but ignored him as she spoke to me. "Hello, Maya," she said as I stepped out of the car. "Lovely Christian Dior."

Okay, she'd redeemed herself. I smiled; that's what I liked—a woman that was on her business and knew who she was dealing with.

"You look fabulous. How are you?" the woman asked. She actually looked like she should be walking on the red carpet herself in a slamming off-the-shoulder black sequined minidress.

"Thank you. And I'm fine," I said.

"Hi, Maya."

I turned to see Cassie, our station publicist, approaching. She had a clipboard and an earpiece, like she was really ready to work. My sometime-bodyguard, Mann, was behind her. He used to go everywhere with me, but I'd slacked off on using him because I really hated always having someone following me. The station had hired him after this stalker situation I'd experienced when I'd first started doing *Rumor Central.*

"Do you need anything?" Cassie asked me.

Different seats, I wanted to tell her. But I had come to terms with my balcony seats. I only hoped that once I got inside and they started taking me upstairs, I didn't lose it. "Just ready to do this," I said.

Cassie gave Alvin a half smile, and then turned and pointed toward the red carpet.

"Okay, Maya, they're ready for you on the red carpet."

She had a sign with my name on it. I guess she needed to hold it up to let the paparazzi know who I was. As if anyone here didn't know who I was.

"Come on, Alvin—this way," I said, taking his hand.

"No." Cassie stopped, a horrified expression across her face. "Th-the red carpet is just for you."

"Excuse me," I said. These people were acting like Alvin was some sort of butt-ugly monster or something. He may have not been all fab, but he wasn't as bad as everyone was trying to make him out to be. And tonight, he actually looked nice. "What about her?" I said, pointing to Cameron Diaz, who was posing on the red carpet with some unknown guy. "She has a date."

"Um, yeah, but that's Cameron Diaz," Cassie replied.

"And I'm Maya Morgan," I shot right back.

"Maya, it's cool," Alvin said. "I'll just meet you in our seats."

I wanted to protest some more, but he squeezed my arm reassuringly as he leaned in and whispered, "It's not that serious. You know this isn't my thing anyway." He gave me a kiss on my cheek and said, "Go enjoy your limelight. I'll be waiting for you inside."

I could barely respond as Cassie shuttled me toward the red carpet.

"Maya!" a photographer yelled out as soon as I stepped out onto the carpet. "Are you here with J. Love?"

I wanted to curse him out, because he had just seen who I was here with, but I kept my smile and ignored his questions as more photographers called my name. I flashed my signature smile as I turned from spot to spot, letting them take pictures of my gown in its full essence, and then I turned around so they could get pictures of the elegant dip in the back of my dress.

"Gorgeous," someone shouted.

"Nice!" someone else said.

"It sure is."

I turned toward the voice and saw it was J. Love. He walked onto the red carpet—no, I take that back. He *strutted* on the red carpet, with a swag that sent the paparazzi into a frenzy and they immediately started hammering him with questions.

"You look gorgeous," he said, ignoring them as he leaned in and kissed me on the cheek.

I tried to maintain my smile for the cameras. But I really

didn't want the photographers taking pictures of us together. "You look nice yourself." And that he did. I thought Alvin had brought it, but J. Love had taken it to a different stratosphere. I could tell his tux was custom, too, but he'd paired it with some Gucci high-top sneakers and a T-shirt. I knew he would definitely make the fashion blogs with that getup.

"So where's your date?" he asked.

"He's inside. Where's yours?"

And then a reporter said, "Yeah, J. Love, where's your date?"

At that point, J. Love turned to the photographer. "I'm rolling solo tonight, folks. If I can't have the one I want"—he looked at me and winked—"I'll just fly by myself."

That, of course, elicited all kinds of chatter as reporters started scribbling on their notepads and the photographers started snapping away.

"What are the chances of you two getting back together?" someone yelled.

"Admit it, you two love each other."

"You guys make the perfect couple," someone else added.

The questions and comments were flying like crazy at us. And all I knew was that I needed to get away. I gave a polite wave as I tried to make my way down the red carpet.

"Wait up," J. Love said, catching up with me.

"I don't want to disrespect Alvin like this," I said through my smile.

"Look at you, trying to have a heart."

"I *do* have a heart," I said. I leaned to his ear and whispered, "And it belongs to Alvin."

"Not for long," he said. "Believe that." The smile left his face and he stared at me to let me know he was dead serious. I had to get away from him. I didn't know what kind of game he was playing, but I wasn't taking part.

"Bye, J. Love."

"What I want, I usually get," he called out after me.

I ignored him, as well as the continued shouts of the paparazzi, as I walked in to take my seat next to my boyfriend—
in the balcony.

Chapter 9

I had just settled in at my desk when Yolanda poked her head into my office door. I was dead tired. The awards show hadn't wrapped up until late last night. Then, I'd had to get up and get to school on time because I had a test in first period. I'd headed to the station right after school. I wished that I could've canceled today's taping. But since that wasn't an option, I was trying my best to just make it through the day.

"Hey, Yolanda. What's up?" I said.

"There is someone at the front desk to see you."

"Who?" I asked, surprised. They knew I was very selective in the visitors I allowed at the station and most people knew not to even bother me. As the host of one of the top TV entertainment shows in the country, I had fans who would try anything to get next to me. So the station usually kept a tight rein on who they let come see me.

"Who is it?" I asked again when she didn't answer.

"Girl, it's your ex."

"My ex?" I said. I knew she wasn't talking about Bryce Logan, whom I'd *thought* was my first love. Bryce knew better than to show up at the station. I had a couple of other exes but none worth mentioning. By the way Yolanda's eyes lit up, I knew exactly who she was talking about.

"J. Love?" I asked.

She nodded with a smirk on her face. "I guess he meant it when he said he wasn't giving you up."

Yolanda had been there when J. Love had first declared he wasn't going down without a fight. And of course, I was sure that she'd heard about his declaration on the red carpet last night since it was all over the blogs today. I'd thought he was just blowing smoke at first because J. Love could have any girl he wanted. I think the fact that I didn't want him only made him want me more.

"What does he want?" I asked her.

"I don't know, but he and his six dozen roses want to see you."

"Six dozen roses?"

Yolanda laughed. "Girl, half the staff is up there going crazy."

I shook my head as I put my pen down and did a quick once-over of myself in the mirror to make sure I was still on point, which of course I was. I made my way up front to find J. Love entertaining Liz, the front desk receptionist.

"And to what do I owe this visit?" I asked as I walked out front.

"Uh, isn't today Valentine's Day?" J. Love asked.

"It's May."

"Oh dang, um, Mother's Day?" he said with a smile.

"I'm not a mother."

"Uh, how about Because Maya Morgan Is Beautiful day?" He looked at Liz. "You like the sound of that?"

Liz gushed like a stupid girl with a puppy-dog crush on someone. "I love it."

"J., what do you want?" I asked, rolling my eyes. He could charm everyone else with that swag, but I wasn't falling for it.

"I just wanted to see what time you get off of work."

"That's why they invented the phone. You could've called or texted." I folded my arms across my chest and gave him a look to let him know that I didn't have time for any BS.

"Since when have I done anything that ordinary folks do?"

"Whatever, J. Love. Again, what do you want?"

"You. You looked beautiful last night. I would've given anything to have had you on my arm. For real."

I pulled him to the side, out of hearing range of Liz's nosey behind. "What's with you? What part of 'I'm in a relationship' do you not get?"

He tried to hug me, but I stepped back, away from his embrace.

"Babe, enough with the charity work. You've proven your point. Now come home to daddy," he said. He tried to seem like he was joking, but I could tell that he really wasn't.

I actually was offended by his words. Alvin wasn't charity.

"Excuse me, you don't know anything about my guy. I'll have you know—"

"Whoa, whoa." He held up his hands. "Before you start going off, I just want you to know that I was just messing with you. I don't mean to disrespect your man. I just wanted to know if you could come with me."

"Come with you where, J. Love?" I asked, exasperated.

"I'm performing at the Grammys and I need a date," he said with a confident smile.

I gave him a serious side eye. *The Grammys?*

"Seriously," he said, reading the doubt on my face. "I'm performing."

Performing? Wow. My mom would so not feel me going to L.A. with J. Love, but how could I pass up a chance to go to the Grammys with one of the performers? *Because you have a boyfriend, that's how,* the little voice in my head quickly reminded me.

"I'm sure you don't have any problems getting a date," I finally said.

"I need a date as fine as you," he said. With a big grin on his face, he continued. "My publicist didn't like me rollin' solo to the Icon Awards. She told me to get someone like Meagan Good or Keke Palmer or even Demi Lovato, but I told her that none of them measure up to you."

"Whatever," I said, rolling my eyes again. I had to give it to him—J. Love had major game, even though it didn't work on me.

"Aww," Liz said. I shot her a look to get out of my conversation.

I turned back to him and let out a long, heavy sigh. "J. Love, I'm in a relationship. I can't be going to your events with you."

"We're friends, aren't we? You can't go as my friend? Come on, Maya. It's good pub for us both."

My hands went to my hips. "So, that's why you want me to go? Because it's good pub for us both?"

"No. I want you to go because you know how I feel about you. But yes, I love the way you look on my arm and you have to admit, I look good on your arm, too."

He was right about that, and I needed something to offset that horrible picture that had been on the front of the *Miami Hot Gossip* magazine this morning. They had gotten the worst-looking picture of Alvin they could find and plastered it all over the cover. It was utterly disgusting.

"Just come as my friend," he continued. "It's a chance to see and be seen in L.A. I mean, I know you're large already, but this is your chance to take it to the next level—I'm talking some Oprah/Wendy type of stuff."

Oprah? Wendy? J. knew just what to say to get to me.

"Let me think about it," I finally said, even though I already knew I was going to try to do everything in my power to go. I just needed to figure out how.

He leaned in and kissed me on the cheek, and then he took my hand and dropped something in the middle of it. "Let this Tiffany necklace help you think about it."

"Boy, I can buy my own Tiff—oh my God, this is the new platinum collection," I said, holding up the necklace. "It isn't even out yet."

"It is for J. Love." He winked, his confidence on full display. "Hopefully, you won't keep me waiting too long. I'll talk to you later." He left me standing there in the middle of the lobby.

As I turned to head back inside, Liz said, "If you don't want the necklace, I'll take it."

I rolled my eyes at her. "I bet you would," I said as I wrapped the necklace around my neck and headed back to my office.

Chapter 10

Today was just a research day at the station, which meant we weren't taping. I was just digging for information. I usually hated research days, but I was actually in a good mood today. I had finally gotten an A on a freaking test. And Alvin had surprised me by paying for my senior portraits. Of course, it wasn't the money that was a big deal. It was the thought. I smiled as I thought of how Alvin was always doing sweet things. Even though he wasn't as rich as J., he was still rich and could afford to buy me whatever I wanted. But it was the thoughtful little things he did that made his gestures so sweet.

You think he'd be sweet enough to let you go to the Grammys with J.?

I quickly shook off that thought. Where had that come from? I'd had a nice time at the Icon Awards with Alvin, even though I'd almost died several times when people noticed me sitting in the balcony. But overall, it wasn't as bad as I'd thought it would be. So, I had convinced myself that I was going to have to pass on J.'s offer, no matter how bad I wanted to go.

I rounded the corner and bumped into Nelly Fulton, a fairly new girl at our school and the winner of the *X Factor* last season. She might have just transferred to our school, but she bounced around here like she was the star of Miami High.

"Oh, hey, Nelly," I said. Nelly was a blond, doe-eyed beauty who reminded me of an edgier Carrie Underwood. She was a pop singer and had been an *X Factor* favorite from the start. She'd captured America's heart with her sob story: an orphan after a tragic accident took the lives of her parents, she was homeless in New York until someone heard her singing and suggested she try out for *X Factor*. Personally, her whole backstory sounded contrived to me, but it had worked and she'd won hands down. I'd heard she had come to Miami High because her record producer and her foster parents lived here and they insisted that she finish high school.

"Hi, Maya," Nelly sang.

"What are you doing up here at the station?" I asked.

"Oh, I'm leaving a meeting," she said with that stupid grin. She always wore that stupid grin.

"What kind of meeting?"

She made a motion like she was zipping her lips. "It's top secret."

I don't know what it was about Nelly, but I wasn't feeling her. She seemed so phony to me. She reminded me of these creatures from this movie I saw called *Gremlins*. They looked all sweet and cute, but would bite you as soon as you let your guard down.

"Wish I could tell you, but I can't," she added.

I bet they were trying to bring some type of singing show to the station for her to host. I'd heard some rumors about that. Whatever, as long as they didn't mess with my show.

"Okay, well, good luck with your meeting," I said, making my way on back to my office. I'd been in the archive room looking for some background information on another story I was working on.

I really couldn't be concerned with Nelly right now. My

research days were supposed to be spent finding stories, and I was starting to bleed my story well dry.

I'd already exposed the cheerleaders at my school for taking part in a little cheerleading escort service. I'd blown the cover off the Bling Ring, a group of kids from my school that used to go around breaking into celebrities' homes. And, I'd gotten to the bottom of a new drug that was sweeping Miami called K2 (that's the drama Travis got me caught up in. Turns out, he was unknowingly selling the deadly drug). But since I'd done all of that, not to mention interviews with all the celebs that contacted me on their own, I'd run some pretty cool stories. I didn't know how I was supposed to keep digging up stories of that caliber. And to be honest, as much as I loved my job, I was starting to feel like that was getting kind of old. I was ready for my next challenge in life. The problem was, I didn't know what that challenge was.

My thoughts were interrupted when I saw Kennedi trying to FaceTime me. I slid the button to connect and said, "Hello, K."

"Hey, what are you doing?" she asked.

"Just working. What are you doing?"

She sighed heavily. "I just got off the phone with Kendrick."

I fought back my groan. Kendrick was Kennedi's ex. She loved him like crazy. She loved him so much, it had made her crazy and she'd found herself right in the middle of an abusive relationship. And Kennedi had turned out to be the main one doing the abusing. Her parents had made her go to therapy because Kennedi had dang near lost her mind behind that boy. I thought she had come to terms with her obsessive behavior with Kendrick, or at least she'd told the therapist that she'd come to terms. But talking with him now couldn't be a good thing.

My silence must've concerned her because she said, "Don't worry. My therapist suggested I call and apologize as a way to heal. So I did. He tried to talk about us getting to-gether, and I turned him down."

"Wow," I replied. "I'm proud of you, girl." I knew that must have been hard for her.

"Yeah, anyway, I was just trying to see if you decided what to do about J. Love. I heard them talking about you on the radio this morning."

I fell back in my chair. "Saying what?" That was the flip side of fame. Everybody always felt the right to weigh in on your life.

"They were talking about how hot J. Love was on the morning show and how he's performing at the Grammys. Are you going with him?" she asked. "Because the deejay said you were."

That made me sit straight up. "He said what?"

"Okay, let me correct that. He said if you had any sense, you'd go. They were joking about how J. Love could have any girl he wants but for some reason he's obsessed with you."

"What does that mean, 'for some reason'? Duh, he's ob-sessed with me because I'm fabulous."

Kennedi laughed, then abruptly stopped. "But are you going, though?"

I sighed. "You know I want to, but . . ."

"But . . . you have a boyfriend. I know." She shook her head. "You're surprising me, Maya. I would've never expected you to give up the diva life to be domestic." She stopped and looked over her shoulder as someone yelled something I couldn't make out. "Girl, that's my mom yelling about some-thing. I gotta go. I'll talk to you later."

She disconnected the video call and left me sitting at my desk, stunned. *Domestic?* My BFF might as well have called me a scandalous trick. Because the day Maya Morgan ever became known as domestic was the day she needed to make some serious changes.

Chapter 11

Libraries just weren't what they used to be. You used to be able to come here and study and read, but this place looked like party central. And the librarian was sitting at her desk, reading a magazine, acting like she didn't see the commotion around her.

For once, I wasn't at the center of the chatter. I was trying desperately to get these makeup assignments done. I'd missed a few assignments that truly could keep me from graduating, and since I wasn't trying to have that, at all, I needed to pull it together.

"Hey, Maya," Nelly said, sliding in the seat across the table from me. This geek named Karrington White was attached to her hip. Karrington could best be described as a goth girl because that's what she looked like with her long black hair and all black clothes. Or at least she used to be known as that. Since she'd started following Nelly around, she'd started dressing like her. Gone were the dark clothes. Now, she wore colorful leggings and some taffeta blouse. When she sat next to Nelly, who had on a chiffon-looking pink dress, they looked like some circus freaks.

"What are you doing?" Nelly asked.

I looked at Nelly, down at my book, then back up at her. "Painting my toenails," I replied.

She giggled. "Girl, you are silly."

"Yeah, Nelly, is there something I can help you with?" I asked. I don't know why she was all of a sudden trying to get buddy-buddy with me, but I wasn't interested. Maybe she wanted me to ask her more questions about what she had been doing at the station. But I wasn't trying to do that either.

"We just don't know each other that well and I just thought we should get to know one another better," she replied. And there went that stupid grin.

"And why would we do that?" I said, not bothering to hide my exasperation.

"You never know," she sang.

"I saw you and J. Love on the Internet," Karrington threw in. Did she just want to feel like part of the conversation? In all four years at Miami High, I'd never held a conversation with this girl. Why in the world did she think I wanted to start now?

"Good for you," I replied.

"I thought you had a boyfriend," Karrington said.

"I do."

Nelly looked confused. "But the blogs said—"

"And you can't believe everything you read online," I snapped. Okay, what was up with this chick? She didn't know me like that. And I didn't want to get to know her either.

"Where there's smoke there's fire," Nelly said, wagging a finger.

Karrington flashed her hands as if she were blowing something up. "Poof! And there are puffs of smoke all over you and J. Love."

I just stared at her. This chick had to be the corniest person I'd ever met.

Nelly leaned into the table. "Aww, come on. You can tell me."

"I can't tell you anything because there's nothing to tell," I snapped. "I have a boyfriend, but what's it to you anyway? You and Nosey Nancy doing a story on me?"

Nelly sat back in her seat. "Maya, do you not like me?" She had the nerve to try and act like her feelings were hurt.

"I don't know you well enough to not like you." I wanted to tell her no, I didn't like her at all, that something about her rubbed me the wrong way. But I didn't want to go there, so I just left it alone.

"Well, I was just wondering if you didn't like me because sometimes it really seems that way," Nelly said.

"Yeah, it seems that way," Karrington added.

I wanted to tell Polly the parrot to shut up. But I just stared at Nelly and said in a straightforward tone, "If I had time to devote to you, I might give it some thought. But I don't, so I don't."

"We were just making conversation," Nelly said.

"Yeah, just trying to talk," Karrington echoed.

I threw my hands up. "Do you two not see that I'm trying to work?"

Both of them looked around the library. "You're the only one working."

"Well, I'm trying to make sure I graduate."

"Oh," Karrington said. "I have a 4.1 GPA, so I'll definitely be graduating. It doesn't matter whether I study."

"And I have a fat bank account so it doesn't matter whether I study," Nelly chimed in and they both busted out laughing.

"I have a fat bank account as well," I said. "But I don't want to be dumb with money."

"Fine," Nelly huffed as she stood up. "It's obvious that you don't want to be bothered."

"And it wasn't obvious ten minutes ago?" I mumbled.

"You don't have to be rude," Karrington replied.

I exhaled. "Look, I wasn't trying to be rude," I said. They didn't faze me at all, but I just wasn't in the mood to go back and forth with them. "I'm just really trying to study."

A smile crept back up on Nelly's face. "All right, we'll let you get back to work. I have a feeling we'll have plenty of time to get to know each other later."

I buried my head back in my book. I had no idea what she meant by that. And right about now, I had no desire to try and figure it out.

Chapter 12

My eyes absolutely had to be deceiving me. No way was that Ross Nixon sitting in the lobby of our TV station. I peeked through the lobby window to get a better look.

"Yolanda," I said, stopping my assistant as she walked down the hall. "What is Ross Nixon doing here?"

She hunched her shoulders. "I guess he has an interview."

"An interview? No one told me that Ross was going to be on the show." Ross was only the hottest up-and-coming young actor in the business. Rumor had it that his latest movie was going to win him an Oscar.

Yolanda shrugged and continued walking down the hall. I guess she felt like she didn't have anything to do with show guests, so she was no help.

I brushed my skirt down, checked my lipstick to make sure the Cherry Red was poppin', then sashayed into the front lobby.

"Ross," I said, greeting him like we were old friends. "It is such a pleasure to meet you. When I heard you were here, I said let me come and greet him personally."

He stood and shook my hand. "Hey, ummm, ummm." He

snapped his fingers like he was trying to remember my name.
Really?

"Maya. Maya Morgan," I said, pointing to the big framed
poster over my shoulder. "Host of *Rumor Central*. You know,
the reason you're here today."

"Ah, yeah, Maya. But there must be some kind of mis—"

Before he could finish his sentence, the double doors
swung open and Nelly bounced into the lobby. Why was she
up here again? "Hey, you," she said, all but throwing herself
into his arms.

He picked her up and swung her around.

"When did you get back in town?" she asked.

"Just landed. Came straight here to see you." He stepped
back and looked her up and down. "Dang, girl, you look
good. Is that the Chanel outfit I bought you?"

She modeled, a big cheesy grin across her face as she
twirled around. "It sure is."

At that moment, I wished that a big earthquake would
come, create a gigantic gap that would then immediately
swallow me up. How was Nelly dating Ross Nixon? And he
was buying her expensive outfits?

"I was just standing here talking to Maya. For some reason, she thinks I'm here for her show."

Nelly giggled as she looked at me. "No, Ross is here to
pick me up."

"Yeah, I'm just here for my boo," he said, pulling her
closer.

His boo?

"So, are you ready?" he asked her.

"I sure am." She tucked a small clutch under her arm,
then turned to Liz, who was obviously eating all of this up, at
the front desk and said, "Can you let Tamara know I'm
gone?" She took Ross's hand. "Oh, and Maya, I don't quite
know how to say this, but it's *our* show now."

"Excuse me," I said.

"*Our* show," she repeated. "You might want to go talk to Tamara about that."

"Yeah," Ross said, grinning hard, "that's what I'm here for. To take my baby out and celebrate her being named co-host of *Rumor Central.*"

"Are you freakin' kidding me?" I shrieked. For some reason, both of them and Liz looked at me in shock.

But Nelly quickly pulled it together and went back to flashing that stupid smile.

"I'm sure Tam will explain everything. Ta-ta." She gave me a stupid finger wave as they walked out the door.

Liz averted her eyes when I glanced in her direction, but I knew as soon as I left she'd be on the phone telling everybody and their mama about the drama that had just unfolded. But I couldn't concern myself with that now. I pushed through the lobby doors, and stomped down the hall, straight into Tamara's office.

"I think I need to fire Kelley, since she doesn't seem to be doing her job," Tamara snapped as I barged into her office.

"And what would her job be? Keeping me out so that I didn't know that you had stabbed me in my back? Again?"

"Okay, Maya. What are the theatrics about now?" Tamara said as she set her pen down and let out a long sigh.

I stood over her desk, trying to contain my anger.

"There are no theatrics unless you want to count stabbing me in the back once again."

She rolled her eyes like I was boring her.

"And do, please, tell me how I stabbed you in the back *this* time."

"Let's see. Nelly Fulton. As cohost? I thought we'd been there and tried that." Tamara had forced my former *Miami Divas* costar Evian Javid on me a few months ago after Evian got kidnapped on spring break. Or, shall I say, pretended to be kidnapped. Turns out Evian was a big, fat liar, had faked the whole thing, and that whole mess had blown up and given the station some really bad press. So, I couldn't believe they were even thinking about trying that again.

"We did try it, and it was actually going pretty well until Evian's little mishap," Tamara said. "We have to keep *Rumor Central* evolving. And even though it didn't work out with Evian, we think Nelly's the one. Her popularity alone is a definite ratings draw."

I couldn't believe this. "Uggh. Shouldn't she be off somewhere making a record or something?"

"That's just it. She actually likes this better and we're more than willing to let her do both. Kinda like Kelly Rowland doing *X Factor*. J. Lo doing *American Idol*."

"This is freakin' insane," I screamed.

She shook her head. "It always is with you, Maya. It always is," she said as she went back to work like she was dismissing me.

I didn't move. I just stood there fuming at her not only doing this, but trying to dismiss me like I was irrelevant. "I'm not working with Nelly Fulton," I snapped.

Tamara glared at me. "And you should know by now, I don't do threats. It's not a good look for you, either."

"Why are you doing this?" I cried, changing my approach. "I bust my butt for this station. I've lost friends, worked like crazy, and you do me like this?"

"Maya, don't beg. It's not a good look."

I glared at her, trying to keep my rage from building.

Tamara's tone softened. "Look, Maya, it's not personal. It's business. Like I said, Nelly has the fan base. They love her. They envy her. And she has the ability to snag the finest guys in the entertainment industry. Did you know she's dating Ross Nixon now?"

"So that's it? Nelly gets to cohost because she has the right eye candy on her arm?"

Tamara gave me a look like she didn't care how crazy that

sounded. "I told you over and over this business is about aes-
thetics."

"What is that supposed to mean?" I snapped.

"It's a total package. People still like you so don't sweat it.
It's just that they *love* Nelly. They want her life."

My hands went to my hips. "So, you're trying to say no
one wants my life?"

Tamara chuckled. "Uh, you said it, I didn't." She stopped
smiling when she noticed the look on my face. "I mean, I'm
sure there are plenty of people that wouldn't mind your life.
Your *professional* life. I don't think anyone is checking for your
personal life." She giggled again.

"Oh, this is real funny to you."

"Maya, calm down. It's not that serious."

She just didn't know. In this game, everything was serious.
"I hope you know what you're doing."

She didn't flinch as she looked at me and said, "Trust me.
I do." She returned to working on her computer, her body
language all but telling me that she was definitely dismissing
me this time.

Chapter 13

I was sick and tired of everybody looking at me like I had three heads. The paparazzi, the people at work, and now, my best friends.

We were sitting in my bedroom, hanging out, shooting the breeze when Kennedi came across a story on MediaTake-Out.com about J. Love's campaign to win me back. Any other guy doing this would've been blasted for looking desperate, but everybody was acting like just because it was J. Love, it was the sweetest thing ever. MediaTakeOut's headline read: J. LOVE DETERMINED TO WIN BACK LOVE OF HIS LIFE. Alvin was going to freak when he saw that.

"I wish you'd stop reading that mess," I told her.

"Hey, I think it's cute how he's going after you," Kennedi said.

I rolled my eyes as I put some polish on my pinky. I usually had my nail tech come do my nails, but I was trying this new nail system and I wasn't doing a very good job at it. "Whatever," I said, blowing a small breath on my nail to try and dry it.

Sheridan leaned in and read the story over Kennedi's shoulder. She had been the main one looking at me crazy lately. She'd seen J. Love's declaration of love on the MTV interview and she hadn't been able to stop talking about it since.

"I just can't believe you're going to pass up an opportunity to go to the Grammys," Kennedi said. I'd told them about my conversation with Alvin and how I'd decided not to go to the Grammys with J. Love.

"For real," Sheridan echoed. "I mean the Grammys are the crème de la crème."

Both Kennedi and I stared at her. "The what?" Kennedi said.

"The crème de la crème."

"What in the world is that?" I asked.

Sheridan shook her head like we were some high school dropouts or something. "It means the pinnacle—the highlight."

"Then why couldn't you just say highlight?" Kennedi tsked.

"Somebody's been studying for the SAT." I laughed.

"Oh, sweetie, I've already aced that," Sheridan said with a smile. "My point is that's the be-all, end-all. The Grammys. And to be center stage at the Grammys? That's a dream come true. And tell me again why you're not going?"

"Because I have a boyfriend," I said slowly. "I don't understand what part of that you guys aren't getting."

Both Kennedi and Sheridan shook their heads at the same time. "Oh, we get it," Kennedi said. "We just don't understand it."

"I don't get it," Sheridan corrected. "I mean, you love the whole fame thing. So much so that you sold your friends out to get it." She tried to laugh, but I knew there was a hint of seriousness. We'd had some major drama behind the stuff I'd put on *Rumor Central*. When I was first hired, Tamara, and the executive producer, Dexter, had wanted more scandal, so they'd convinced me to reveal dirt on my friends—everything from cheerleading escorts to a bling ring. It was a big mess and I'd vowed never to go digging for dirt in my own backyard again.

"Sheridan has a point," Kennedi said, stepping in before I had time to get an attitude with Sheridan. "Are you that in love with Alvin that you're ready to let the fame go?"

"I don't understand why I can't have both," I protested.

"Because your business is all about perception. You're the cool kid. The diva everyone wants to be like. Girls all over the world aspire to be like you. To date guys like yours," Sheridan said.

"That is, as long as that guy isn't Alvin," Kennedi added, as the two of them busted out laughing like they had really said something funny.

"I really can't appreciate you guys talking about my man," I said, frowning to let them know this was no laughing matter.

Their laughter died down. "Chill, don't get all sensitive. You know we like Alvin, but we're just being real," Sheridan said. "Besides, you've been complaining all evening about them bringing Nelly on to cohost your show. What kind of press do you think she's going to get dating Ross Nixon? You need some positive press."

I knew that, but what was I supposed to do?

"I mean, of course I want to go to the Grammys," I finally admitted. "But how am I going to do that when I'm with Alvin?"

Kennedi shrugged. "I don't know, but I'd be trying to figure out a way."

"I know," Sheridan said, snapping her fingers like she'd just come up with a great idea. "Alvin really is a sweetheart. If he knows you want to go, he won't mind you going."

"Yeah, right," I said. That was her solution? "He already told me he wasn't feeling J. Love."

"No, seriously," Sheridan replied, getting excited like she'd really figured something out. "Just hear me out. All you've got to do is just ask him."

"I'm not about to come right out and ask him that," I replied. I wouldn't be able to ever look him in the face, asking some mess like that.

We sat thinking for a moment, then Kennedi said, "I know. Why don't you send a text and make it out like you were going to send it to me or something, but you send it to him instead. Like it's a mistake. And the text could just say how much you really want to go to the Grammys, but you don't think Alvin would understand and how there's nothing going on with J. Love, but you just really want to go."

"Like he's going to buy that," Sheridan said, turning up her lips.

"Do you have a better idea?" Kennedi asked. Since Sheridan shut up, I guess that meant that she didn't.

I thought about what Kennedi was saying. Alvin *was* a sweetheart and if I could convince him that nothing was going on between me and J., maybe I could work this out.

"Okay, I can get with that," I told them, nodding. "That may be just what I need."

"Thank you, and that'll be two tickets to the after party," Kennedi said with a big grin.

"The Grammys are in L.A.," I replied, finally smiling.

"That's okay, we'll fly out," Kennedi said.

"We sure will," Sheridan replied.

I laughed. My girls had come through for me. Now, I could only hope that everything would work out as easy as they thought.

Chapter 14

I stared at the text again, trying to get up the nerve to press SEND. But for some reason, this was a whole lot harder than I thought it would be. I knew seeing this text would hurt Alvin, but I really and truly didn't know what else to do. Nelly was moving in fast on my territory. I could try to take the high road all I wanted, but I was in the business of branding and I was starting to wonder if everyone was right that Alvin was bad for my brand.

I hadn't been able to get that hunk Ross Nixon off my mind. How Nelly had pulled someone like that was beyond me. Granted, she was cute and all, but Ross was major.

I glanced over at the tabloid magazine Tamara had handed to me on my way out the door today. Nelly and Ross were hugged up, and I'll admit it, they looked good together. And if Ross was bringing up her stock, were my friends right? Was Alvin bringing mine down?

"Stop procrastinating and send it," I mumbled. I read the text one more time.

> Girl, I don't want to hurt Alvin but the station is threatening to fire me if I don't go to the Grammys w/J.
> What am I gonna do?????

I exhaled, pressed SEND, and waited. I knew Alvin was at home. He'd called me about thirty minutes ago and told me he was in for the day.

On cue, not even a full five minutes later, my cell phone rang.

"Hello," I said, trying to sound upbeat.

"Hey, Maya, what's going on?" His tone was measured like he was weighing his words.

"Nothing, babe. Just on my way home from the station," I chirped. "What are you doing?"

He paused. "Reading this text that you must've been trying to send to one of your girls."

"What?" I said, sounding shocked. "What are you . . . OMG. I . . . that . . . oh, wow. That wasn't meant for you." I hoped that I sounded convincing.

"Obviously," he said. I could just picture him pacing back and forth across his living room.

"Alvin, I am sooo sorry. I didn't mean to send that to you," I lied.

"So, the station is talking about firing you if you don't go on a date with your ex?"

"Alvin, oh my God. I—I, no, let's not talk about it."

"No. I want to talk about it," he demanded. "They're seriously talking about firing you?"

I sighed, trying to act like I really didn't want to say anything. "It's the Grammys. J. invited me to be his guest—for publicity purposes," I quickly added. "You know how Tamara and the other producers keep trying to tell me that I need to do stuff for the *Rumor Central* brand. They think me going to the Grammys would be good PR."

"So, going on a date with your ex is good PR?" he said, like he couldn't believe what I was saying.

I felt really bad, but I'd come this far. I had to see it all the way through. "It's not even like that."

"So, what is it like then, Maya?"

I didn't say anything.

"Do you want to go?" he asked pointedly.

I still didn't say a word.

"Answer me, Maya!"

His tone made me jump.

"Okay, yeah, of course I want to go to the Grammys."

Silence filled the phone. "Then you should go," he finally said.

"Really?" I said, a little too excitedly.

"Wow," he replied like he was stunned by my excitement. But he exhaled, then said, "Yeah. Really. Since this is obviously something you want, go for it."

I wanted to jump for joy. That was why I loved Alvin. Most guys wouldn't be this understanding. I wanted to chitchat with him some more, but now that I knew I was going to the Grammys, my focus needed to be on looking fabulous. I needed to get off the phone with Alvin so I could call J. Love and let him know. Then I needed to begin planning so that I could take L.A. by storm.

Chapter 15

This is the life that I was meant to live. I loved covering the red carpet, but I loved *being* covered on the red carpet a whole lot more.

"Maya! J. Love!" Paparazzi and reporters were yelling our names from every direction. And as if we were completely in sync with one another, J. Love and I turned and smiled.

He was right about one thing. We made an awesome couple.

J. hadn't seemed surprised when I'd called and told him I would go—almost as if he'd known without a doubt that I'd give in. So, this past week had been filled with beauty appointments—nails, spa, hair, shopping. Of course, my mom wasn't having me going off to L.A. with a guy, but then she had the not-so-brilliant idea to come with me (just another excuse to go shopping in Beverly Hills if you asked me). I didn't sweat it, though, because she was super excited and had found me the perfect gown in a Rodeo Drive boutique, had them overnight it, then had alterations done in twenty-four hours. She was making sure everything was on point for my Grammy debut.

"Are there plans to tie the knot?" someone shouted from the crowd of media people.

"Wow, can I get out of high school before you start trying to marry me off?" I joked.

"Yeah, I'm not the marrying type," J. Love said. "But if I were to get married, it would definitely be to someone like her." He smiled and pulled me closer, and the paparazzi ate it up. If Tamara and the others were worried about my stock, this should definitely bring it back up.

"Right this way," our escort said when we reached the end of the red carpet.

I let J. lead me into the coliseum, to our seats on the third row. I was no groupie, but if I was, I would've done a little dance when they sat me down with Pharrell on one side of me and Kevin Hart on the other.

"Hey, what's up, J.?" Pharrell said, standing and greeting J. Love.

I did a little wave at him as J. Love dapped him. "It's all you," J. replied.

"Congrats, man. I heard Hype Lee was directing your new video," he said.

J. nodded. "Yeah, that's a big deal."

"I still need to holla at you about that collaboration," Pharrell said.

"Oh, you don't have time for me," J. Love joked. "You too busy being happy."

"I make time for you, my man," he replied.

They laughed and joked some more. J. spoke to several other celebs and introduced me to a few, before taking his seat. I loved how J. Love just commanded a room. People respected him everywhere he went.

This would definitely be a night to remember. I think the best moment came when J. Love finally took the stage. He gave a performance that rivaled Usher and Chris Brown's much-talked-about previous performances. He was on point and I sat there smiling like I was his proud girlfriend or something.

"He was so good," the girl behind me leaned up and whispered after the crowd had given J. Love a standing ovation.

"Thank you."

"You two make such a cute couple."

All I could do was flash her a smile.

After J.'s performance, we went to a commercial break and someone with an earpiece and a clipboard came over and lightly tapped me on the shoulder.

"Miss Morgan, Mr. Love requests your presence backstage," the man said.

I smiled proudly as I followed the man backstage. There was a lot of activity going on backstage, and I almost passed out when I passed Beyoncé in the hallway. But I wasn't about to be a groupie, so I just said, "Hey, how are you?" as I passed.

She gave me a genuine smile and replied, "Fine. Thank you," before disappearing around a corner.

"In here," the man said, motioning for me to go into an oversized dressing room.

"Hey, you," I said, tapping on the door.

There were several people in there, including a few I recognized—his business manager, his publicist, and a few of his boys.

"Hey, I would've brought you back earlier, but I wanted you to see it from the audience," J. Love said as a sound guy removed his microphone from under his shirt.

"No, you were fantastic," I said.

He leaned in and kissed me, and it actually caught me off guard.

"Thank you for coming here. You made this night special."

"No, thank you for having me. I'm having a wonderful time."

"Did you see Shaun Robinson from *Access Hollywood* outside?" he asked.

"No, what is she doing out there?"

"She wanted to interview us. She said everybody is loving us. So much so, that the people at *Essence* want to put us on the cover of next month's—"

"J. . . ."

He held up his hand. "But we're not going to talk about that right now. I told her we'd get with her later, but I told you, girl. Me and you are so good together."

I just stood there and smiled.

"Next year you're going to have to make sure you're here, because I know your boy will be nominated, not just performing. My album didn't drop in time to make this year's nominations."

I had no doubt not only would he be nominated, but he'd win.

He hugged me again, and said, "All right, baby, let's get changed then we can go and enjoy the rest of the show."

"So, did you enjoy yourself?" J. Love said as we sat in the back of the car heading back to the hotel. I really wished that I could stay in L.A., but it was finals time and I didn't have a choice. I was on the first flight out in the morning. What was so jacked up was that my mom was staying a few extra days to shop.

"I did. I had a nice time. So, thank you again for inviting me." I slipped my stilettos off.

"I told you. Did you see the way everyone ate up our appearance?"

"Yeah, we do make a cute couple." I smiled at him. "Too bad we're not really a couple."

He looked at me in all seriousness. "Well, that can be changed."

"Come on, J. . . ."

"*I know. I know. You got a man,*" he said, singing a popular line from one of his chart-topping songs. "You know how I feel about you. But I'll keep it strictly business. I can do that because I know that sooner or later, you'll come around."

"Whatever."

He flashed that cocky expression. "I told you, I always get what I want." Before I could protest, he changed the subject. "But I did want to talk to you because I want you to be in my new video, the one Pharrell was talking about."

I struggled to contain my excitement. "Seriously?"

"Yeah, the studio is pumping a lot of money into this record. It's my new cut, 'A Love Like This,' mixing some old-school beats, with the new-school flavor."

"It sounds like it's gonna be hot."

"It is, but I know how we can make it hotter."

"How?"

"Have you as the star. We had Taraji, but she got a movie she's shooting and I thought who's as hot as Taraji? And it dawned on me that I knew someone hotter."

My eyebrows raised. Taraji was quite hot for an old woman, but of course, I was hotter.

I leaned back in the seat. A video?

"I'm not a video vixen, you know?" I felt the need to re-mind him.

"Of course I know that. I just want you to take the part. So what do you say?"

A video? I was just complaining about *Rumor Central* and wanting to try something new. While I'd never want a career as a video girl, it might be fun to do.

"You know, I think I'd like it," I finally replied.

"You know, I know you would," he said. He pulled me

closer to him and I couldn't help it, I snuggled in closer. "I told you, girl, you and me together . . . we can conquer the world."

I don't know why, but his words actually made me sad. Maybe because a part of me felt like he was right and since my heart belonged to another, there was nothing I could do about it.

Chapter 16

It was about to be some major drama in my relationship. When Alvin called me today and simply said, "Are you back home? I'm on my way," I knew things were about to get ugly. I'd gotten home from L.A. early this morning. J. had wanted me to stay, but I was down to the wire with the grades. I'd struggled through the day and was so tired. I just wanted to get home and rest, but it didn't look like I'd be resting any time soon.

"What's up?"

He refused to say anything else or answer any questions and I knew this wasn't going to be good. I glanced down at the *Miami Hot Gossip* magazine. The headline screamed at me: BACK IN LOVE.

J. Love and I were snuggled up together in the cover photo like we truly were in love. I knew that's what had my boyfriend on fire. The minute I'd seen the picture this morning, I'd known there was going to be trouble. I didn't even remember when it had been taken, but we were definitely all up under each other like we truly were back in love.

The doorbell rang and our maid, Sui, made a beeline to get it. But I jumped up.

"I got it!" I snapped.

Sui just shook her head at me and turned and walked out the room. Luckily, Sui had been with us long enough to mind her own business, so she headed back upstairs without saying a word.

I swung the door open. "Hey," I said, trying to be perky and smiley. I was still tired because of that early-morning flight. I'd gotten to school in time for my fifth-period final and then I'd come straight home, hoping I could rest before having to deal with this mess.

Alvin didn't say a word as he pushed past me.

"Well, hello to you, too," I said, losing my smile.

He spun around to face me and waved the rolled-up *Miami Hot Gossip* magazine in my face. "Seriously, Maya?"

"What?" I said, playing dumb. I took the magazine, opened it up, then acted like I was just as shocked as he was.

"Don't try to act like you haven't seen this. You've been at school all day. Somebody told you about it. You could've called me and warned me."

"I haven't seen it. I don't know anything about this," I said, defensively.

"Whatever, Maya." He pointed to the table behind me. "So, why is the magazine sitting over there?"

I shrugged. "I don't know. Sui reads that mess. I hadn't had a chance to look at anything. Why are you trippin'?"

He thumped the magazine. "You're really gonna ask me why I'm trippin'? My girl is on the front of a gossip rag with her ex with a headline that reads, 'Back in Love.' You don't see anything wrong with that?"

I wanted to tell him that he needed to remember who he was talking to and lower his voice, but I knew the picture was bad and he was pissed, so I was going to give him a pass.

"Since when did you become jealous?"

"Since my girl started blatantly disrespecting me," he snapped.

Sometimes, I missed the nerdy Alvin. He'd always shown me that he had a little *umph* in him. But since we'd officially gotten together, I'd seen less of that and more of the do-whatever-I-say Alvin.

"It's no big deal. You know how the media is," I said.

"Yeah, I know how you guys are," he said. "But you gave them the ammunition."

"I didn't have anything to do with this."

He opened the magazine to the centerfold picture and shook it at me. "Look at your face, Maya. Look how you're looking at him. You look like you're in love."

"That's called acting," I replied. Alvin was right. The picture was so out of order. I didn't even remember taking it. "Look, I'm really sorry. I wasn't trying—"

"Why do you need to act like you're with someone else when I'm supposed to be your boyfriend?" he asked, interrupting me.

"I was just playing it up for the cameras." I sighed, but I really wasn't in the mood for arguing. I was exhausted and the last thing I felt like doing was arguing with my boyfriend.

Alvin stopped and stared at me.

"Do you love him, Maya?"

I cocked my head as my mouth dropped open. "Are you really asking me that?" I asked. "Of course I don't love him. I'm just playing a role."

"Yeah, at my expense."

I huffed as I plopped down on the sofa. This conversation was getting real old. "You told me you were okay with me going with him to the Grammys."

"I was okay with you going to the Grammys. I wasn't okay with this!" He waved the magazine again.

"You do know this is all part of what I do?" I said, glaring up at him and wishing I could make him disappear, at least until he calmed down.

He was silent for a minute before saying, "Well, I don't know if I can handle this anymore."

That made me stand up. "What is that supposed to mean?"

He tossed the magazine at the table and tried to flex. "Meaning, I'm sick and tired of you and your ex, and you're going to have to show me some respect."

"Are you threatening me?" I stepped closer so he could look me in my eyes.

He didn't flinch. "Take it as you want. I'm just telling you. There will be no more outings with your ex." I immediately thought about the video J. wanted me to do. That I *wanted* to do.

I sighed, then turned and walked away. "You're really overreacting," I said.

"You heard what I said." That made me raise both eyebrows. Alvin was about to get straight cussed out.

"Uh, I don't know who you think you're talking to, but I'm not the one," I snapped. Forget being nice. Yes, I was wrong, but I wasn't about to let him talk to me crazy.

He sighed, too. "Look, Maya, I'm sorry. I'm not trying to be a jerk, but I'm just really pissed."

"Okay, but you're pissing me off, too. I know you're used to saying whatever you want to your girl, and she takes it," I said, referring to his ex, Marisol. That crazy chick had tried to kill me, literally. She'd run me off the road trying to get me away from Alvin. She was out on bail, pending her trial, but as far as I knew, she was off minding her business. She'd loved Alvin something crazy. And although I'd never seen Alvin talk to her crazy, she was so weak and passive when it came to him. So, she'd let him get away with it. Me, on the other hand . . .

"I chose you over Marisol, so we don't even need to talk about her."

"Oh, don't act like you did me a favor," I snapped.

He exhaled in frustration. "That's not what I'm saying at all."

"So what are you saying? Because Marisol was your little puppet and you could say or do whatever, you think you can say whatever you want to me?"

"Now who's overreacting?"

I pointed a manicured nail in his face. "Don't get it twisted, Alvin. I'm still Maya Morgan."

"Yeah." He stared me down but didn't flinch. "And all Maya Morgan cares about is maintaining her star status. You all up under your ex bothers me. That should mean something. But you're right. You're the diva, but I'm starting to think maybe Maya Morgan might need to be by herself," he said, then turned and stormed out of my front door.

I didn't know how to act. In the year since I'd known him, Alvin and I had never had so much as a minor disagreement. Now, we were having something this major? I let him go, and my gut told me if I didn't clean up this situation with J. Love, things with Alvin were going to go from bad to worse.

Chapter 17

I was not a happy diva. I mean, I didn't know what kind of attitude they expected me to have, sitting in this conference room like I was supposed to be excited about everything that was unfolding.

They were acting like the *Rumor Central* ratings were horrible. Yes, they'd dropped a little, but I was still at the top of my game, so why they felt the need to change things, I just didn't know.

I sat on one side of the conference table; Nelly sat on the other. Tamara was at the head. Dexter and a few of the other producers filled out the other seats.

Tamara had been rambling for a few minutes, but I'd been too mad to even focus on what she was saying. I finally decided to tune in.

"I know everyone is not exactly thrilled with the changes, but we always try to do what's in the best interest of the show," she said. "MTV has a show coming out to rival *Rumor Central* so we have to solidify our place in the marketplace before it hits the air." She turned in my direction. "Maya, your stories have been slacking off. We need some more Bling Ring, some more escort stories. We need some hard-hitting dirt."

I didn't bother to respond. I wish I would sell out another friend for these backstabbing people. *Get Nelly to do it*, I wanted to say, but I remained quiet.

Tamara continued talking, turning now to Nelly. "Nelly, we are so happy to have you on board. We'll be expecting you to develop some contacts and bring in hard-hitting stories as well. We also hope your fan base will bring a whole other element to the show."

"Not to mention that dynamic personality," Dexter said, patting her hand. I started to throw my phone and hit him in his red mop head. He used to be a fan of mine. That showed there was no loyalty in the entertainment business.

"When are these changes taking place?" I asked, finally speaking up. I needed to prepare myself and figure out my game plan.

"We're not sure, but we're at least a few weeks out," Tamara replied. "We want to do heavy promotion, but we want it out before the MTV show and that comes out in August."

I sat back in my chair, relieved that I had a minute to figure things out.

"We really want to get some A-list celebs to help us promote the revamped *Rumor Central*," Tamara said. "You think Ross will do a promo?" she asked Nelly.

Cue stupid grin. "Yes, he'll do anything for me."

"Maya, you think you can get Alvin?" Dexter said, snickering as the whole table busted out laughing.

I just glared at all of them. "Real funny," I said.

"Come on, guys. Let's remain focused," Tamara said, fighting back a laugh herself.

Nelly raised her hand like we were in class.

"Yes, Nelly?" Tamara said.

"Can I say something to the team?"

"Of course."

She stood like she was putting on a performance. "Well, let me just say I am thrilled to be on board. I have been a fan of the show, and just the thought that I'm now a part of it makes me so happy. I'm going to give my all to take *Rumor Central* to the next level."

I could tell they were all eating her phony act up. Was I the only one that could see through that sham?

"Thank you all so much for working with my schedule," Nelly continued. "The album is a little delayed, but I want to assure you all that I remain committed to *Rumor Central.*"

"And what do you all plan to do when Britney Spears here goes on tour?" I asked.

Tamara shot me a look of disdain. "We've worked all that out. You'll handle the show solo on those days and, Maya, when and if you have anything come up, Nelly will handle it."

Oh, I didn't miss her dig at me. *When and if,* like I didn't have a life. I was so sick of these people.

I tuned them out and pulled my phone out to continue a conversation I'd been having via text with Kennedi earlier. I'd filled her in on my fight with Alvin yesterday and I'd been unable to answer her last question because the meeting had started.

Just wish Alvin was hot. Then all my troubles would be solved, I typed.

"Maya, are we interrupting you?" Tamara asked.

I quickly pressed SEND, then set my phone back down. I'd pretend to pay attention, but I wasn't trying to hear anything they were saying. I had no intention of being Nelly Fulton's partner, and as soon as they gave me her start date, I would start making plans to leave.

As soon as we walked out, Nelly came skipping over to me. "Maya."

I kept walking like I didn't even hear her.

"Maya, you know you heard me call you," she said.

I spun around to face her. "What do you want?"

"We're going to have to get along," she said. "I'm willing to try if you are."

I just stood staring at her. "What do you want from me, Nelly?" This girl had to be the most annoying person I'd ever met.

"Your friendship."

"I don't need any more friends."

She shook her head like I was a lost cause. "Look, I think it would be great if you and I could get with some of the celebs they were talking about and shoot some of the promos. I mean, you've met Ross. I'm sure he wouldn't mind. And I've met J. Love at a few industry events, so I'm sure he would do it, too. Although I don't know him personally. You know, maybe me, you, and him can hang out, go to dinner or something so he'll feel comfortable endorsing the show."

This girl was truly crazy. "Not gonna happen."

"Why? Are you guys together, like boyfriend-girlfriend?"

"You know what? My personal life isn't any of your business. I have to see you at school. I have to tolerate you here, but I don't have to be your friend. I don't *want* to be your friend."

She had the nerve to sigh like she was getting really frustrated with me. "I don't know what kind of working relationship you expect us to have like this."

I threw my hands up in frustration and walked away. She just didn't know—we would have no working relationship. I needed to figure out a way to nip this cohost idea in the bud before it even got off the ground.

Chapter 18

I didn't have a choice. I had taken today and just chilled. I'd even passed on going to the mall with Sheridan and Kennedi. I still hadn't recovered from the L.A. trip, then that exhausting sham of a meeting yesterday. Not to mention the argument with Alvin—all of it had worn me out. I'd hoped he'd come around, but it was almost ten and I still hadn't heard from Alvin, nor had he answered my calls or texts.

I took a deep breath, my cell phone gripped tightly in my hand. I knew what I needed to do to fix this. I knew what I would want Alvin to do. Even still, that didn't make it easy.

"Just do it," I mumbled to myself, before tapping J. Love's name and waiting for the number to dial.

"What's up, beautiful?" he said, picking up the phone on the first ring.

"It's all you," I sweetly replied.

"I was just about to text you a pic of these fly Louboutins the stylist got for you to wear in the video. They're custom made."

"Custom-made Louboutins?" I squealed. I quickly caught myself and fell back on my bed. "Actually, J., that's what I was calling about. I'm not going to be able to do the video."

"What?"

"It's causing too much drama." I felt sick even as the words left my mouth.

"Too much drama with who?"

"With my boyfriend." I sighed. "He feels disrespected and I don't want to upset him."

J. Love groaned. "Come on, Maya. Everything else aside, this is business. You can't let ol' boy mess with your business."

"Ol' boy is my boyfriend," I replied, "and he doesn't want me to do it."

"Wow. Since when does Maya Morgan like being told what to do?"

I had to tell myself that J. was just trying to get me riled up so I had to take what he was saying with a grain of salt. "I don't like it. It's called respect, J. If I was in a relationship with you and you didn't want me to do this, I'd respect you enough not to do it."

"And I'd respect you enough not to ask you some mess like that," he quickly replied. "I would realize that you're Maya Morgan and anything that can further your career is good for you."

"Oh, so being a video vixen will further my career?" I tried to laugh to ease the tension.

He didn't find anything funny. "First of all, you won't be a video vixen. You are the main chick in the video, the love interest, the female star. And second of all, since MTV is doing a world—did you hear me, *world premiere*—yeah, it can further your brand."

I was quiet. I hadn't known this was going to be a world premiere. "J., I just don't want drama in my relationship."

J. Love took a deep breath, like he was trying not to get upset. "I don't want drama, either, babe. But this is what I was talking about. This is why people outside the business don't work. You get me and I get you. I know this is all business, babe. But it's cool. If you don't want to do it, I'm not gonna sweat you. Your girl Nelly wants the part anyway."

"What?" That made me sit straight up in my bed.

"Yeah," he casually replied.

"Why didn't you tell me?"

"Cuz it didn't matter. The job was yours. But now . . ."

I couldn't believe it. This girl was like a fly, always buzzing around my picnic. First my job, now my side jobs! "So you would really give my spot to Nelly?" I asked him.

"I wouldn't *give* it to anybody. The casting director would. I only had one request. Maya Morgan. If I can't have her, I don't care who they get. As long as she's hot."

"Nelly is not hot," I snapped.

"Says you."

I was fuming. That's why that trick was asking me all those questions. So, now, not only was she trying to weasel her way onto my show, but she was trying to slither her way in good with my ex. "Really, J.? That's how we playing it?"

"I'm not playing anything, Maya. You're making your choice to stay home and be little Holly Homemaker or something. So you let your nerd boyfriend keep his leash around your neck and do whatever he needs to do. I'll holla at you later."

Before I knew anything, J. had hung the phone up.

"Ugh," I screamed, tossing my phone across the room. J. Love was the only guy with the nerve to talk to me like that. No, he *used* to be the only one, I told myself. Now, apparently, Alvin felt like he was calling some shots as well.

Was J. Love right? Was I letting Alvin put me on a leash?

No, I was just trying to respect my boyfriend. That's it. And I was going to stand by my decision, no matter how much it killed me.

Chapter 19

As soon as I stepped outside of my last class, I saw several people talking as they pointed down the hall.

"What's going on?" Sheridan asked, meeting me in the hallway.

"I have no idea," I replied.

We made our way down the hall, to try and see what everyone was looking at. The entire hallway was filled with heart-shaped balloons.

"Dang," Sheridan said. "Somebody is having a lucky day."

I moved my messenger bag to my other shoulder, stood on my toes, and strained to get a better look. Suddenly, I heard singing, and a guy stepped through the middle of the balloons. He was singing "I Must Be Crazy" by Tyrese. His voice actually sounded really good.

"Wow, someone really messed up," a girl said.

Everyone looked around to see who he was singing to. Then to my surprise, he kept walking until he stopped right in front of me.

"Maya Morgan, I have a message for you," the guy said.

"It's okay. I can deliver my own messages." I turned to see Alvin coming up behind him and my mouth dropped open.

"I just came to say I'm sorry." Alvin handed me a huge heart-shaped balloon with the words *Forgive me* written across the front.

"Dang, nerd boy got game," this annoying boy named Jock said.

"Shut up, Jock," Sheridan snapped.

"He's gonna get in trouble for having all these balloons in the hallway," our student council president, Lee, threw in.

Alvin ignored them all, as if he and I were the only ones in the hallway.

"What are you doing?" I whispered, even though everyone was zoomed in on us and could make out everything I said.

"I hate when we fight and I just wanted to say I'm sorry," Alvin replied.

"Awww," someone said.

"Why she always get the good ones?" someone else added.

I smiled. The good ones. Alvin was a good one and I did hate fighting with him.

He finally noticed all the people staring at us. He leaned in and whispered, "You know I don't like all this attention."

"So, why such a public apology then?"

"Because you know how much I hate the limelight, and I thought if you saw me doing something so public, you'd know I was serious."

"Excuse me, what is all of this?"

We all turned to see the assistant principal, Mr. Jacobs, approach us.

"Sorry, sir," Alvin said. "We'll clean it all up." He motioned toward the guy who had been singing, and he immediately began gathering up the balloons.

"I know school just dismissed, but we can't have these kinds of distractions," Mr. Jacobs warned.

"Yes, sir. We're on it."

Mr. Jacobs nodded his approval as he turned to the other students. "Nothing to see here, folks. Unless you're helping clean this mess up, I suggest you all head on home."

Of course, no one was trying to help so most of my classmates scattered and walked away.

"What are you about to do?" Alvin asked me.

"Nothing. We were just going to go get something to eat," I said, pointing to Sheridan.

"Do you mind if I steal her from you?" he asked her.

Sheridan smiled as she shrugged. "Do your thang."

Alvin took my hand and led me out to his car.

"What was that all about?"

He stopped right outside the passenger door. "I told you that I hate fighting with you. And I miss us. And if you want to do the video, then I'm not going to trip."

I shook my head. "No, I won't do it if it bothers you that much."

"No, if you're my girl, then it's no reason for me to be all worked up and upset. I trust you, so why I was trippin', I don't even know."

"Yeah, I don't want him." I leaned in and lightly kissed him. "You are the love of my life so all that extra stuff was unnecessary."

"Aren't I allowed to mess up?" He flashed an apologetic grin. "It's not like I do it often."

He was right. Alvin was one of the good guys. "All is forgiven." I smiled, happy to have the Alvin I knew and loved back.

Chapter 20

I had to admit it, J. Love and I put the awesome in awesomeness. Alone, I was fabulous; together, J. and I took fabulousity to a whole other level. Too bad I was in love with someone else. J. Love could proclaim his love for me all he wanted. My heart was somewhere else. And tonight, I was simply playing a role.

The studio had laid everything out. We were filming on South Beach today and one of the scenes called for me to rock a bikini. But I told them I didn't do hoochie because the last thing I wanted was to be lumped into the same category as all these video vixens around here so they'd settled on a sexy sundress.

A woman who looked like she was somebody's assistant approached us as we walked into the studio. "Good afternoon. Right this way, Mr. Love, Miss Morgan," she said.

We followed the woman inside the huge building, which looked like it used to be an old warehouse. But it had been updated with all modern décor. People scurried around, setting up lights, barking orders, and moving equipment. Several dancers were in a corner, rehearsing. I was feeling the whole vibe.

The woman led us down a long, concrete hallway. She stopped in front of an oversized dressing room. "You gon' be all right?" J. Love asked me.

I nodded. "I'm a big girl," I told him. "And I'm not new to this."

Just then, an Amazon of a woman with a wild honey-blond afro approached us. She looked like she was in desperate need of a grilled cheese sandwich or something, she was so skinny. Even still, she was stunning and looked like she needed to be on a Paris runway.

"Hey, I'm Charlie Rose. I'll be doing your makeup," she said.

"*The* Charlie Rose?" I asked, shaking her hand. Charlie Rose was one of the best makeup artists and stylists in the business. She'd been the stylist for everyone from Oprah to Beyoncé.

"The one and only," she said with a pleasant smile.

"Didn't I hear that you had been swept away to Milan?" I asked.

"Honey, they swept me right back." She giggled. "They wanted nothing but the best for Mr. Love here."

"And she's definitely the best so hook her up right." J. leaned in and kissed me on the cheek. "I'm gonna go get ready myself."

He headed out and Charlie patted the chair in front of a long floor-to-ceiling mirror. "All right, let's get you started. Karli is going to work on your hair," she said, motioning to the lady adjusting several curling irons on a table.

"Hi, Karli, do your thing," I said, sitting in the chair.

I sat down and an hour later, I emerged with full fabulous curls, makeup to die for, a tight royal-blue spaghetti-strapped jumper and my Louboutins.

I made a memo to myself that the station would need to fly Charlie in for special events for me because this girl was bad.

"Dang, I didn't know you could improve upon beauty," J.

said once I approached the set. He looked amazing in a plain white tee with a blinged-out design, a black Armani blazer, and baggy jeans.

The shoot took a while because we had to shoot and reshoot scenes over and over. J. was doing an extended version with a storyline. I was the scorned lover who he didn't appreciate until I was gone. It was exhausting work, but I had so much fun.

By the time the crew started wrapping up, I was still hyped. J. Love met me in my dressing room. "So, how was it?" he asked.

"It was everything!" I replied, slipping my Louboutins off.

"Yeah, it can be grueling doing the same thing over and over, but I love it," J. replied. "And wait till you see the end results. Hype is no joke," he said, referring to the director.

"I can tell," I replied.

"Guess what, though?"

"What?"

"Hype loves you and wants to talk to you about casting you in this new movie that he's directing and I'm starring in."

"Movie?"

"Yeah, I told you. Stick with me and we'll conquer the world!"

I laughed. "I would love to do a movie, so I'd definitely have to talk with him about that later." I held up my shoes. "Hey, so what do you want me to do with the shoes?"

"They're yours."

"Oh, wow, I get to keep them?"

"Girl, don't nobody want to walk after you," he joked.

"Whatever. My toes are cute." I wiggled my foot.

"They sure are." He looked at me all sexy for a minute, then relaxed and said, "We're all going out to celebrate. So, let's go."

I glanced down at my phone and saw two texts from

Alvin. It was late, but I'd promised him that I would swing by his place after the shoot.

"I, um, kinda have plans," I stammered.

J. looked at me like I was crazy. "Plans? Girl, we just wrapped an award-winning video shoot in one day. That's cause for celebration. We got to go have some fun."

Before I could reply, my phone rang. I looked down and saw Alvin's number. "This is my boyfriend."

J. didn't seem fazed. "Okay, and? Tell him you're still at work. Tell him the shoot is running long if you don't want to tell him you're going out."

"I don't like lying."

"Oh, come on, Maya. Really?"

J. Love was right. I was ready to relax, let my hair down and have a good time. I could hang out with Alvin any time.

I sighed and answered on the last ring before it went to voice mail. "Hey," I said.

"Hey, you. How are things going?" Alvin asked.

"It's going well."

"I was wondering if you were wrapping up. I was hoping we could still meet up. I can come there and we can go grab a late dinner or something."

I eyed J. Love, who was standing there like he had no plans to move. I turned my back to him and lowered my voice. "Yeah, um, I think it's going to take us a lot longer than I expected. We're nowhere near finished." I actually felt awful lying to Alvin, but "Hey, I'm going to party with my ex and his crew" didn't sound like it would fly.

Alvin was quiet. "Oh, okay."

"So, I'll just catch up with you tomorrow," I said. "Okay?"

More silence. "All right. Good night," he finally said. "I love you."

I looked back over my shoulder at J. Love. "Me, too," I responded.

I hung up the phone and turned back to J. He was standing there with a stupid grin on his face.

"You might not like lying, but you sure are good at it."

My mouth dropped open. But before I could say anything else, he said, "Girl, chill, I'm just messing with you. Come on, let's go have a great time!" He grabbed my hand and pulled me out the door.

Chapter 21

"Go, Maya, it's your birthday! You gonna party like it's your birthday!"

The crowd chanted while I did something I never in a million years thought I'd be caught dead doing—twerking. And not just regular twerking, I'm talking Rihanna, Miley, and Beyoncé rolled up into one.

"Okay, okay," I said, the minute I noticed someone with a camera phone. "I'm done."

J. Love turned to the guy filming, one of the dancers from his crew. "Man, put that camera up! We trying to just have a good time."

"See, this is why I sit over here, minding my business," I said as I walked off the dance floor.

"Awww, come on," J. said, pulling me back to him. "I shut him down. We're having a good time. Don't ruin it."

"Tell your boys don't be filming me. I don't want to end up twerking on WorldStarHipHop," I snapped.

Just then, the music slowed and Trey Songz's "Heart Attack" filled the room. I tensed up as J. Love pulled me close to him to slow dance.

"You don't want to dance with me?" he asked when he noticed how stiff I was.

"J. . . ."

"Just relax," he said. "We're just dancing."

I took a deep breath, then laid my head on his shoulder. I couldn't help it. It felt good to be so close to J., so when he squeezed me tighter, I squeezed him back.

"You know, I really enjoyed seeing you let your hair down," he whispered. "You don't do that enough."

"I have an image to maintain."

"So do I. And together, we look like two celebrities having fun. That's all. No big deal."

"I did have a good time tonight," I said. "Except for that wine cooler."

He let out a small laugh. I had finally broken down and let J. talk me into drinking a wine cooler. And it had me buzzing, a feeling I did not like.

I actually had been completely against it, but I'd gotten caught up in the moment, with all the fun we were having.

"So, Maya Morgan, are you really happy with nerd dude?" he asked me as we slowly swayed back and forth.

"Nerd dude's name is Alvin, and why did you ask me that?"

"I just asked a question."

"Alvin is a good guy."

He stopped, pulled back and looked me in the eye. "That's not what I asked you. Are you happy?"

I thought for a minute, then said, "I am."

He didn't crack a smile as he said, "Then why are you here with me?"

That made me stop swaying and I took a step back.

He pulled me back toward him. "You know I keep it real. You are here because you're feeling me, just like I'm feeling you. Maya, we are good together."

"We tried that already, J.," I said.

"Yeah, and I messed up. I thought you had sold me out to the tabloid and I just screwed up. I need you to give me another chance."

"I can't, because I'm with someone."

"So, you said."

"So, I am."

"Okay, cool then."

I raised an eyebrow. "Just like that?" J. Love didn't give up on anything that easy.

He pulled me back to him to finish our dance. "I don't believe in harassing anyone, but you will be mine. In the meantime," he continued, "we're just going to relax and have a good time." He eased my head back down on his chest and I closed my eyes and savored the moment.

The flash of a bulb caused me to jolt up. A photographer was zoomed in on us, snapping away.

"Man, get them out of here!" J. yelled to his bodyguard.

"Dang," I said, huffing because I didn't want any pictures.

"You know that's the price of fame." J. shrugged. "But tonight, I just want to enjoy my time with you before we have to return to reality and I have to return you to your man. Because you know he's only borrowing you right now."

"Whatever, J." I told myself that he was only kidding, but for some reason, the feeling in the pit of my stomach told me that he wasn't.

Chapter 22

The ringing phone blared, startling me out of my sleep. I fumbled on my nightstand, grabbed my phone, and put it to my ear.

"Hello," I mumbled. I had no idea what time it was, but the sun was peeking in through my closed blinds.

"Must've been a long night."

"Oh, hey, Alvin," I said, rolling over on my back. I massaged my temple. How could one wine cooler make my head hurt so bad?

"Your video shoot ran long, huh?"

"Yeah, yeah." I tried to focus while struggling to hold in my groan. See, this was exactly why I didn't drink. Who wanted this awful feeling?

I put my hand over my eyes. "It ran a lot longer than I thought it was going to."

"That's funny because it looked like to me you wrapped up pretty early, then went out to celebrate."

"Huh?" That woke me up and I bolted right up in my bed.

"Yeah, you know, you told me you weren't anywhere near

finished at nine o'clock. But at nine-forty-five, I see pictures all on Instagram."

"Wh-what?" I knew that we had taken a lot of pics last night, but Alvin wasn't even on Instagram.

"Oh, so now you don't know what I'm talking about?" I could hear the attitude all up in his voice.

"Alvin, why are you calling me this early tripping?"

"First of all, it's not early. It's noon. Secondly, I'm not trippin'. I just can't appreciate being lied to."

I didn't know what to say, so I just said, "I didn't lie. We just wrapped everything up and went and hung out."

"So you wrapped everything up minutes after talking to me?"

I was fully awake now. I swung my legs over the edge of the bed and moved the phone to my other ear. "Seriously, Alvin?"

"I'm just saying, when I talked to you, you said you guys were going to be there all night."

I sat on the edge of my bed and massaged my temples some more. My head was throbbing and Alvin was making it worse.

"What is this, the third degree?" I snapped. "And now you're checking up on me on Instagram? You don't even have an account, so what? Did you log onto someone else's account to try and spy on me?"

"I didn't need to," he replied. "Someone saw it on Instagram and sent it to me."

"Why is somebody worried about what I'm doing? Who was it?"

His silence was my answer. That couldn't be anyone but his whack, desperate ex-girlfriend, Marisol.

"Tell your ex to get out of my business before I have her thrown back in jail," I said.

"I'm not concerned about Marisol. I'm concerned about

my girl. Who lied to me and said she was working when she was really out kickin' it with another dude."

"I wasn't kickin' it with another dude," I said. "I was with a bunch of people from the set."

"Whatever, Maya. I saw the picture. Dude was all over you."

I let out a heavy sigh. "You know that's for the camera."

He huffed. "No, I don't know anything, except I told you that I'm getting real tired of this."

"When did you become such a drag?" I huffed. "You never used to trip like this."

"Because I never used to be disrespected. I don't know if you think being a nerd, as your friends call me, makes me weak, but I'm not the one."

I wanted to scream. "Nobody said you were weak, Alvin. Geez!"

"Keep on playing me if you want to, Maya. I am a nice guy, but don't push me."

Before I could reply, he slammed the phone down.

First, J. Love had hung up on me, now Alvin. Tamara was right, I was starting to think I wasn't cut out for this relationship stuff.

Chapter 23

Since my former *Miami Divas* costar, Evian Javid, had been exposed as a liar, she'd tried to stay pretty clear of me. Mainly because she knew that I could've ruined her. We had been all set to put her on blast on *Rumor Central* and I hadn't done it. I'd felt sorry for her, so I'd taken up for her on the air, explaining why she'd faked her own kidnapping, how desperation sometimes drove people too far. I made people feel sorry for her. Because I played it like that, the story died down and the spotlight didn't stay on her long.

But the fact that she pretty much kept her distance from me was a silent acknowledgment that she appreciated what I had done. Which was why I wasn't understanding why she, Bali, and Shay were standing in my face right outside of my sixth period.

As usual, the ghetto-fabulous Shay was the spokesperson for the group. Shay's father was a big-time NBA player. He might have money, but it didn't give him class. And his daughter was just as hood. She and I had a love-hate relationship. Oh, who am I kidding? We couldn't stand each other.

"What's up, Maya?" Shay asked as they blocked my path.

"Are you guys here to harass me? Because I'm really not

in the mood," I said. I'd had to do a Skype audition today for Hype and while I'd done okay, I didn't feel like I'd done my best. I think it was because I was so distracted with all the drama in my life.

"Girl, nobody cares about your mood," Shay replied, tossing her blond braids. "That's not why we're here."

"Then what do you want?" I asked.

"We heard about them bringing in Nelly on *Rumor Central*," Evian said. Her voice was soft, almost like she wanted me to know they were coming in peace.

I folded my arms and waited for them to gloat because I was sure that's what they were about to do.

"And we just wanted to see if there's anything we can do to help," Bali said. He swung his blond bangs out of his face. As usual, he had on tight skinny jeans and a designer top. Bali always was so extra with everything. His father was a Cuban bigwig so they had more than enough money to keep him looking fab. But, Bali had a knack for staying in trouble.

"Really, Bali?" I said. The bad part is Bali and I used to be the tightest of us all (next to me and Sheridan). Like the others, he had been upset when they'd fired the *Miami Divas*. Then, he'd gotten really mad because I'd done the story on the "Bling Ring" on my show. Bali had been among several people taking part in the Bling Ring, breaking into celebrities' homes and stealing stuff. Bali didn't steal anything, but he'd gone along for the thrill and so he could film it all. He'd given me one of the videos a long time ago, and after we fell out, I used the video on my show. After my story, Bali's dad had been so mad that he'd sent Bali back to Cuba to live with relatives. But that hadn't lasted long and Bali was back to finish the school year.

"Really," he said. "We're trying to help you out."

That definitely made me laugh because the day these three wanted to help me with anything was the day I knew something was truly wrong.

"We don't like you," Shay felt the need to clarify.

"Okay, and?" I said.

"But there's one person we like even less than you," Shay said. "And that's that Pop-Tart Nelly."

Evian stepped up. "Do you know she called Bali a freak?"

That got him riled up all over again. "And you know if my dad hadn't threatened to deport me if I got into any more trouble, I would've stomped that heffa down," Bali said, his neck wiggling like crazy.

"Okay, but what does any of this have to do with me?"

"Well, we know you looked out for Evian," Shay continued, "so we wanted to look out for you, give you a piece of information."

Bali clicked his teeth. "Watch your back, diva, because Nelly is not only out to be a cohost. She's out to take the job completely and get you fired."

"How do you know that?" I asked. As if she even could.

"I heard her telling that little jackrabbit sidekick of hers how she'd told Tamara people were talking about you like a dog because of Alvin. She also said she got someone she knows to write a story blasting you at *US Weekly*."

I was speechless. Oh, she was playing dirty for real? "Why are you guys telling me this?" I said, still trying to understand their motive.

Shay looked me dead in the eye. "There's a part of me that said, 'Let her get fired, it would serve her right,' because you did us real dirty."

"I'm sorry," I said for the thousandth time.

Shay continued, "But Sheridan got us to see that any one of us would've done the same thing if we'd been the ones they offered the job to."

I couldn't believe after all this time, they were finally cutting me some slack.

"Wow. Well, thanks for the info."

Bali gave me a once-over. "You going a little soft, diva. You best to get it together, before that trick has your job and your man. She looks innocent, but it's those that you have to watch the most."

The bell rang, letting us know we were late for our seventh-period class. "Thanks, guys. I'll keep you posted."

We all walked off at the same time. Had I been under-estimating Nelly? Whatever, I thought. She might try to get dirty, but she was no match for me in that department.

Chapter 24

June 6 couldn't get here fast enough. That was graduation and I was so ready to bid farewell to Miami High. I was so tired of the hate from these busters at my school. Like now, I was minding my business, trying to piece together my behind that had just been chewed out by my world history teacher. As if her grueling exam wasn't enough, she had to make me stay after class and hear her lecture about not living up to my potential, riding my fame. Whatever.

Add to that the ugly fight I'd had with Alvin two days ago (and the fact that we hadn't talked since then) and my annoyance meter was off the scale.

"May I help you?" I snapped, looking at two girls who kept staring at me as I made my way into the lunchroom. I wasn't in the mood, and if they said the wrong thing to me, they were about to feel my wrath. Luckily, they quickly darted off in the opposite direction.

"Hi, Maya." I couldn't help but roll my eyes as Nelly and Karrington came bouncing over to me.

"Hi, Maya," Karrington echoed.

I didn't speak as I kept moving through the line. I thought

about what Bali, Shay, and Evian said. Nah, they were reading too much into things. This girl was so ditzy. She might be able to sing, but that was about all she had going for herself. I wasn't going to worry about her at all.

"Maybe she's mad about the picture in the magazine?" Karrington said. I know she wanted me to ask what picture. I wouldn't give them the satisfaction.

"Good-bye, Nelly and no-name," I said.

"Oooh, somebody didn't take their happy pill today," Nelly sang.

"Maybe she can take some personality lessons from you," Karrington chimed in.

"Maybe you can get your nose up out of her behind and get your own life. Jerk," I told her.

"Maya, was that really necessary?" Nelly asked. She looked ridiculous, in a ballerina tutu and a one-shoulder spandex top. I know she was trying to go for the whole unique pop star look, but she just looked like she was trying way too hard.

"Nelly, is it really necessary for you to talk to me at all?" I snapped as I snatched up my tray and walked away. These people were so working my nerves.

I scanned the cafeteria for Sheridan and Kennedi. I spotted them in the back in our usual spot and I made my way over.

"Hey," I said, sliding into the seat across from them.

"Hey," they both replied as they exchanged uneasy glances.

"What's up with you guys?" It was then that I noticed several other people staring at me as well. "What's up with everybody?"

"You okay?" Sheridan asked.

"Umm, yeah. This stupid world history exam just kicked my butt. As if I need to know what the capital of Turkey is. When will I ever use that information again?"

They just stared at each other, then me.

"Okay," I said, setting my water bottle down. "Somebody needs to tell me what's up."

"You obviously hadn't seen today's *Miami Hot Gossip* magazine."

"No. Why?" I rolled my eyes. "Oh, let me guess. They have pictures of me and J. Love? Yeah, someone posted them to Instagram, now Alvin is trippin'."

Neither of them said anything as Kennedi slid the magazine across the table. "Umm, you might want to see for yourself."

I groaned as I flipped the magazine open. "What page is it on?"

"Page sixteen," Sheridan whispered.

I side-eyed her. "It ain't that serious. It's just a stupid picture of me and J. Love."

"It isn't J. Love," Kennedi mumbled just as I got to page sixteen. My heart fell into the pit of my stomach as I read the headline: CAUGHT CREEPING. And right underneath it was a picture of my boyfriend, Alvin, kissing Marisol. The kiss itself cut me to the core, but knowing he'd kissed her after she'd tried to kill me made me sick to my stomach.

I looked up to see both Sheridan and Kennedi staring at me like they were scared that I was going to go postal.

"Th-there has to be some kind of explanation. Maybe this was taken back when they were together."

"That's what I thought at first when I saw it," Sheridan replied. "But it's at that new yogurt shop on Biscayne. The one that just opened last week."

I hadn't thought my stomach could drop any further, but it did. That place had just opened up, which meant my boyfriend was cheating on me.

"I'm sure there's a reason," Sheridan said. Even as the words came out, it didn't sound like she believed them.

"Girl, don't try to sugarcoat that," Kennedi said. "There is no reason for your guy to be kissing all up on his ex-girlfriend."

Kennedi was right. There was nothing that could explain this.

"You dang near throwing your career away for this dude and this is how he repays you?" Kennedi snapped.

I felt tears welling up, which was not good because Maya Morgan didn't cry over a guy.

"I'm gonna go," I said, standing.

"You need to eat," Sheridan said.

"I'm suddenly not hungry." I had to hold it together because several eyes were still looking in my direction. Nosey folks.

"Are you okay?" Sheridan asked.

I nodded. I was going to call Alvin because he was going to tell me something. He was going to explain this to me. I had no idea what he could possibly say, but he had to tell me something.

I left the lunchroom and headed to my car because I didn't want any of these nosey people eavesdropping on me.

As soon as I sat in my driver's seat, I called Alvin. I wanted to scream when it went straight to voice mail. I hung up and texted him.

Call me. Asap.

I noticed the date and remembered that he had some meeting this morning, but he'd better call me right away. I was about to call him again when my cell phone rang.

I looked at the caller ID and groaned.

I answered the phone and asked, "What do you want, J?"

"Well, hello to you, too," he said.

"Sorry. I'm just not in a good mood."

"Yeah, I kinda figured that. I saw the magazine and well, I'm shocked. I mean, you trying to do right by him and this is how he repays you?"

"So, you're calling me to gloat?"

"Come on, baby girl, you know me better than that. I was just calling to check on you and see if you need me to take ol' boy out or something."

That made me smile. J. Love acted tough, but he really was a suburban kid from Jacksonville, Florida. There was nothing hard about him. "No, I don't want you to take him out," I replied. "Besides, you're not really a thug. You just play one on TV."

"Yeah, you right about that. I'm a lover, not a fighter. But I know people who know people."

I tried to laugh, but I choked up. I caught myself, inhaled, then said, "I can't believe this, but I'll handle it."

"What did he say?"

"What can he say?"

"Well, just know if you need anything, I got you," J. Love replied.

I wanted to tell him that I might need him to keep his calendar clear because if this turned out to be true, and not some sick Photoshop job, Alvin was as good as gone.

Chapter 25

I had snatched up my phone so quickly when I saw Alvin's number, I didn't even get a chance to say hello.

"Okay, who died?"

"You're about to," I replied.

"Seriously, Maya?" Alvin said, exasperated. "I'm in the middle of this important meeting and you're blowing up my phone, having the secretary come and get me, and nobody's dead for real?"

"Not yet anyway."

He had the nerve to act irritated. "Maya, what are you talking about? I really don't have time for this."

"Oh, but you have time to be sitting up kissing on your ex-girlfriend?"

Silence filled the phone. Then, he said, "What in the world are you talking about?"

"Hold on a minute."

"Maya, I don't . . ."

I couldn't even hear the rest of his sentence because I pulled the phone away from my ear. I don't know why I didn't think of this in the first place. I opened the magazine up, snapped a picture of the page and texted it to him. "Check your phone," I told him.

"I'm on my phone. Why can't you tell me what this is about?"

"Because I can show you better than I can tell you. Check your phone," I repeated.

"Hold on," he huffed. I could hear him fumbling around and then silence again.

"Hello?" I said.

"Maya, it's not even what it looks like." Oh, his entire tone changed now.

"Don't tell me it's not what it looks like, because it looks like you're kissing on your ex-girlfriend. But I know better than that. Is it Photoshopped? It *better* be Photoshopped," I said, before he had a chance to answer.

"I wasn't kissing her. She kissed me and it caught me off guard," he replied.

"Whatever, Alvin," I yelled. "This doesn't look like you were caught off guard."

"Can we talk about this when I get home?"

"No, we can't! We're gonna talk about this right now!"

He let out a heavy sigh. "Maya, I don't want Marisol."

"I can't tell."

"Regardless of what it looks like, it was nothing."

"You are so full of it, you liar!" It was taking everything in my power not to cry. Out of every guy I had ever dated, Alvin was the last one I ever thought would cheat on me. "How could you do this to me? And with her, of all people? She's about to go on trial for trying to kill me. You freakin' turned her in. And now, you're out playing kissy-face with her?" I screamed.

"Maya, I have to go back in this meeting. I'll be there to meet you after school so we can go somewhere and talk."

"Alvin!" But before I could say another word he hung the phone up. I wanted to scream. Oh, he could try and meet me all he wanted, but I wouldn't be going anywhere with him. Ever again. If I didn't have a presentation in my last class, I'd leave right now.

I don't know how I made it through the rest of the day, but I did and as soon as that seventh-period bell rang, I hightailed it out of there. I wanted to be gone before Alvin got here, but of course he was leaned up against my car.

"Move," I said.

"No. Not until you hear me out."

I folded my arms across my chest. "You know, Alvin, there's nothing else to hear. *Miami Hot Gossip* heard it all."

"No, they didn't, because if they did, they would've seen me afterward, pushing her away and asking her what in the world was wrong with her."

"Tell that to somebody else. You must think I'm boo-boo the fool."

Just then two girls passed by me snickering. "Dang, she took him back already," one of them said.

"Why don't you mind your own business?" I shot them an evil glare.

"Oh yeah, look who's talking about minding their own business?" the girl said, rolling her eyes.

"Whatever." I turned my attention back to Alvin. "Do you know what kind of fool you've made me look like?"

He just stared at me like he was trying to see through me. "Yeah, the same kind of way that you made me look."

"Oh, don't even try to compare the two. I wasn't locking lips with my ex. You can try to dress it up however you want, but everyone at school was looking at me like I was some poor desperate chick who was done wrong by her man."

"So that's what this is about? How you look?"

"You're doggone straight that's what this is about!"

"So it's cool with you if I was kissing her as long as no one saw it and made you look bad?"

I was about to go off, but I saw a few other people looking my way, so I just stepped closer to him and lowered my voice. "Oh, don't you dare try to turn this around on me. I'm the freaking laughingstock of the school!"

"And of course we can't have that," he said, his voice full of sarcasm.

"No, we can't!" If he was trying to make me feel bad, it wasn't going to happen. "I have a brand."

He threw his hands up. "Oh yeah, your brand. That Maya Morgan brand. The brand is why you had to go to the Grammys with another guy. The brand is why you had to play me in order to go because you weren't woman enough to come right out and tell me how bad you wanted to go."

"What are you talking about?" Could he have known I sent the text on purpose?

"Whatever, Maya. You're trying to play innocent, but you're not."

"So that's what this is about? You kissed your ex-girlfriend because I went to the stupid Grammys Awards with someone else?"

"Not *someone*—your ex-boyfriend who's made no secret he wants you back. Do you know how that made me look? Oh, and let's not forget you lied to me about a video I didn't want you doing in the first place."

"First of all, you're not my daddy so you don't tell me what I can and can't do. Secondly, nobody cares how you look! Everybody cares how I look!" The words left my mouth before I even realized it and my tone softened. "I didn't mean it like that. I meant—"

He held his hand up to stop me from talking. "No, that's exactly what you meant." He blew a frustrated breath, looked around the school, then shook his head pitifully. "You know what, Maya? You're right. I'm not about that life. I've loved you from the moment I laid eyes on you, but it was never enough. I kidded myself into believing that it ever could be. I could have all the money in the world, but I don't have the status you and your friends have and that makes me a nobody. So you go find you a somebody to be happy with."

"What? What does that mean?" I stared at him and turned my nose up. Was he breaking up with me? "Are you dumping me?" I asked.

He let out a pained laugh. "Yeah, I'm done. But we can say it was a mutual decision because I know for you, the only thing that matters is the spin. I'm sorry about the pictures in the magazine. They really are not what they seem, but I don't think that matters to you anyway. You wanted an excuse to get out, so you're out."

He walked away without giving me a chance to say another word. Not that I could have anyway. I was stunned silent. How had he been the one caught cheating . . . and I ended up being the one who was dumped?

Chapter 26

I flushed the toilet and dragged myself back into my bedroom. My mother had been in here three times already, probably because she wasn't used to me being sick. Although I wasn't physically sick, I had called in sick to work and taken a day off from school. I just couldn't do it. When I told my mom that I had broken up with Alvin, she said I was heartbroken, but Maya Morgan didn't get broken up over a guy. Especially one that had cheated on her.

But if that was the case, why had I not been able to pull myself out of bed all day except for just now and only because my bladder couldn't hold it anymore?

I was just about to crawl back into my bed when someone knocked on my door.

"Ms. Maya?" It was Sui, our maid.

"What?" I grumbled, pulling back my covers.

"There's someone here to see you."

"I'm not here."

"But he's seen your car, and he knows you are."

"*He?* You tell Alvin I have nothing to say to him, and who let him past the guard?"

"Um, it is not Mr. Alvin. It is a man by the name of Mr. Love?"

J. Love? What was he doing here? He'd been calling me all day, but I'd turned my phone off because I didn't feel like talking to anyone.

"Well, tell him I don't want to talk to anybody," I said.

"Well, you're going to talk to me," I heard J. Love's voice say.

"Mister, mister. You cannot be up here," Sui said, frantically. "Miss Maya is not allowed to have male visitors in her room."

"I'm not in her room," J. Love said. "I'm standing out in the hallway with you. Maya, I need to talk to you."

"Go away, J. My dad shoots guys who come in my bedroom."

"But your dad isn't here."

"Oh no, oh no," I heard Sui mumbling.

I decided I needed to go out before she had a heart attack. I made my way across my plush bedroom carpet and swung my bedroom door open.

"Dang!" J. said, making a face. And then I realized my hair was probably all over my head and I didn't have a drop of makeup on.

"Oh my God," I said, closing the door real fast. "Give me a second," I snapped. I grabbed my brush and tried to make some semblance of order out of my hair and then I dabbed some powder across my face, put on a touch of lip gloss, and then opened the door back up. Sui was still standing there, ringing her hands. J. Love had a determined look on his face like he wasn't going anywhere.

"Okay, much better," he said, smiling. "Now go put on some clothes so we can go."

"I'm not going anywhere with you, and what gives you the right to come barging in my house demanding to see me?"

"Because word on the street is that you're sitting up in here going crazy and that you were a basket case at school yesterday, called in sick today, and now everyone's mumbling that you've been dumped and don't know how to take it."

"What?" I said.

"Exactly," J. Love replied. "And divas don't roll like that, right? Isn't that what you're always telling me?"

"Are people really talking about me?"

"Yeah, I'm sure MediaTakeOut probably has a long scope lens trying to get in your house and get a picture of you now. Don't let them see you sweat," he said. "Don't let them see that somebody got the best of Maya Morgan."

I stood taking in his words.

"If ol' boy cheated on you, then it's his loss and better you find out now than later."

Those words made me choke back a sob, and before I knew it, I was crying.

"I just can't believe he did this."

J. Love took me in his arms. "It's okay, babe. I told you I'm here for you. Now the best way to get him back is to get yourself together. Let's go out on the town. You put a smile on your face and let him see you in a magazine with another dude."

"But he knows that we're not together."

"And he also knows that I want you," he said matter-of-factly.

"J. . . ."

"Naw, I'm not saying you gotta give me a chance right now," he said, holding his hands up. "But make him think it. Make him suffer like you're sitting here suffering. Come on, Maya, you're better than this," J. said, motioning up and down my body.

Even though I was wearing silk bottoms and a tank, I had

wrapped myself in my big Hello Kitty plush robe with some giant furry house shoes. Yeah, there was definitely nothing diva about me right now.

"You know what? You're right." I dried my eyes and held my head high. "This ain't how divas roll," I said, pointing up and down my body.

"That's my girl," he said. "Let's get changed. I'm waiting."

Sui lightly tapped him on the shoulder. "But can you please wait downstairs? I would hate for Mr. Morgan to get home and there be a murder."

"She has a point," I said. "Give me fifteen minutes."

"Okay, that means thirty." He winked. "But I'll wait, because you're worth it."

As soon as he left, I jumped in the shower. The cold water instantly gave me a much-needed jolt. J. was right. Maya Morgan didn't do pity parties, especially over a guy who didn't deserve it. That's what I got for turning "domestic." I was turning my focus back to what mattered. My fabulous life.

"Wow, you were actually ready in twenty minutes. You look gorgeous," J. Love said when I emerged downstairs, fresh, dressed, and back to normal. "That's the Maya Morgan I know."

"Thank you." I smiled. "So where are we going?"

"How about we go to McCormick and Schmick's?"

"Okay, cool," I said. For anybody else, that may have seemed like a big deal.

"I got us a private room," he said.

"A private room?" I said. "What do we need a private room for?"

"To celebrate."

"What are we celebrating?"

"Oh, dang, that's the whole reason I came over here." He pulled his cell phone out and punched in a number. "Oh hey, yeah I'm here. I forgot to call. . . . Yeah, she is. . . . Okay, hold on."

He handed me his cell phone.

Who is it? I mouthed. He thrust the phone toward me without answering. I finally took it. "Hello?"

"Maya Morgan?"

"Yes," I said.

"Hey, lady, this is Hype Lee, the director."

"Oh, hey," I said, looking at J. Love in confusion.

"Yeah, usually this should come through your agent, but J. is a friend of mine so I wanted to deliver this news to you personally."

"What news?"

"I'd be honored if you would take on the female lead in my new film."

"What?" I said. "I got the part?" I hadn't even done a formal audition, just sent him a video tape of me reading lines.

"Yes, ma'am. I told you we wanted a fresh face on the acting scene. And with your star power, we can't go wrong. We already sent our formal offer to your agent so he should be calling you about it soon, but I'm hoping you'll say yes."

Yes! I wanted to scream, but I knew I had to play it cool and I had to make sure the contract was on point.

"Wow! Thank you. I'm honored and I can't wait to see the contract."

"All right, I'll talk to you soon." He hung the phone up and I handed the phone back to J.

"Why didn't you tell me that immediately?"

He shrugged. "I wanted to cheer you up."

"Well, that definitely cheered me up! I can't believe I got the part!" I jumped up and hugged him tightly.

"Girl, please, as if you didn't think you would."

"I'm not an actress, remember?"

"You're a natural at everything you do. And me and you together, girl—we're about to take celebrity couples to a whole 'nother level."

"But we're not a couple," I reminded him.

"Not yet. But we will be." He grabbed my hand and led me out before I could respond. The thing is, this time, I didn't want to protest.

Chapter 27

Something was seriously wrong with Yolanda. She stood in the doorway to my office, looking like she'd seen a ghost.

"What's wrong with you?" I asked, spinning around in my chair. I was in a much better mood today. I had gotten the part, J. Love had taken me out and shown me a fab time, and by the end of the night, I was like Alvin who?

"Um, I was just, um . . . um, I was bringing your scripts," she stammered.

"Okay, thank you," I said, holding my hand out for her to give them to me. She didn't move. "Okay, Yolanda. What's going on?"

She took a deep breath, then let out a long sigh. "You're not going to be happy."

"What are you talking about?" Yolanda could be so extra sometimes. I grabbed the stack of scripts and began flipping through them.

"What are we doing some kind of story that—" I stopped when I saw it. Right underneath my name in parentheses to give the show intro was another name.

"What the . . . ?" I mumbled, as I flipped through the

pages. The stories on today's episode were alternating: I read one and then Nelly read one. "What is this?" I screamed.

Yolanda shrugged and said, "They just gave them to me to give to you and I just happened to notice that—"

I didn't even give her a chance to finish before I jumped out of my seat and bolted out of my office. I stormed into Tamara's office and her secretary, Kelley, immediately jumped up and tried to stop me. "Maya. Maya, wait."

I ignored her as I continued toward Tamara's office. I probably should've brought the issue up with Dexter since he was the show producer, but Tamara was the main boss, so no sense in me wasting my time with a peon.

"Maya, she's not in there and—"

I spun around and stared at Kelley. "Where is she?"

"She's . . . she's unavailable."

"Where is she?" I screamed, when it seemed like she didn't want to tell me.

"She's in Nelly's office."

Nelly has an office?

I had been down this road before with Evian not too long ago. I wasn't about to travel down it again. I walked into the office to see Nelly and Tamara giggling like they were best friends.

"Excuse me," I said. "Tamara, can I talk to you?" I completely ignored Nelly.

"Hi, Maya," she said all bubbly. I wanted to smack her in her eye. Yes, I knew they had been talking about bringing Nelly on board, but no one told me this would be happening today.

"Aren't you excited?" Nelly continued.

"No, because I didn't know anything about this," I said, glaring at Tamara.

Tamara glared right back at me. "Well, if you bothered responding to my voice mail and if you hadn't skipped our meeting, then maybe you'd know what was going on."

I folded my arms across my chest. "I've been busy!"

"Okay, then I guess you'll find things out when everyone else does."

"Now, now, ladies," Nelly said. "We're family now. All of us."

I ignored Happy Hannah, and said, "Tamara, what's going on?"

"I told you that I would be hosting with you," Nelly said. "Did you not believe me?"

"Haven't we tried this before?" I asked Tamara, still not even acknowledging Nelly.

"You know what? I'm gonna let you two chat." Nelly headed toward the door. "But don't chat too long, Maya. We have a show to do!" She hurried out the door and I wanted to pick her swivel chair up and throw it at her.

"Are we really doing this again?" I asked Tamara as soon as Nelly was gone.

"This time will be different," Tamara replied.

"Well, I'm not doing it."

Tamara exhaled in exasperation. "Maya, you've worked with me long enough to know that I don't do threats and I don't do ultimatums."

"I'm not threatening. I'm just saying, if she stays, I don't, and I don't do ultimatums either."

I expected Tamara to get an attitude right back, but she actually smiled. "Maya, it's really not that serious. We're just trying to revamp things. Stop being a spoiled brat and get out there and do your job before I sue your little behind for all the money your daddy has!"

That caught me off guard because Tamara had been pretty cool with me.

"Maya, you need to get on set. They're calling for you," Yolanda said, poking her head in Nelly's office.

I happened to glance over at the big screen monitor that sat across from Tamara's desk. Nelly was already in place. I rolled my eyes, not saying a word as I stomped out of her office.

"That's what I thought," I could've sworn I heard Tamara mumble.

Oh, this battle was far from over. I wasn't about to go down this road again. Last time I just threatened to quit if they gave me a cohost. This time, I was actually going to do it.

"Maya, come on, we're thirty away," the director, Manny, said, frantically waving for me to hurry up.

I scurried on to the set as Manny began counting down.

"We're on in five, four, three, two . . ."

"What's up, everybody? It's ya girl Maya Morgan," I said, reading the teleprompter and forcing my signature smile. And while I had every intention of staying professional, I knew today was just the beginning. Things were really about to get crazy around here at *Rumor Central*.

Chapter 28

I was trying to have a good time at this party, but I wasn't even going to lie. I was completely bummed out. I couldn't believe that Tamara had played me like this and that I might really have to make good on my threat. The show had actually gone off without a hitch. As far as I could tell, no one could see I had an attitude on air, but off air, it wasn't pretty.

Of course, I didn't really want to quit *Rumor Central,* but I'd threatened to walk away so many times that if I didn't stay true to my word this time they weren't going to take me seriously. And I had to show them I was serious. Nelly may have had them fooled, but I was hip to her game. She was straight trying to play that nice role, but I had no doubt that that chick was a backstabber if I ever saw one.

"You sure you don't want to dance?" a guy asked me.

"Do you see me here with somebody?" I snapped.

He looked around. "No."

And that only made me madder. J. Love had all but dumped me since we got to this party. I'd told him I didn't want to come, but it was for one of his boys who had a new album out and he said we really needed to start getting as much press together as possible. But since we'd arrived, he'd been MIA. Now granted, I got it, it was probably because I'd been sitting there with a stank attitude. The last words he'd said to me before getting up and walking away were, "You probably should've stayed at home. I'm going to walk around."

But I couldn't help it. I was in a foul mood. I sat there, sipping my cherry limeade, trying to will myself out of my funk.

"You sure I can't get you anything to drink?" the waitress asked.

I'd told this chick fifteen times I didn't drink. Why she was trying to force Patrón down my throat was beyond me.

"No, thank you," I replied.

"Okay, just checking."

I'd had enough. A change of attitude wasn't working. I was going to find J. Love. He needed to take me home. I couldn't help but wonder where he was. It's not like J. Love was a dancer so I didn't expect to see him on the dance floor, but after walking around the club for ten minutes, I saw no sign of him. I had just turned and headed back to the VIP section when I saw him on the dance floor, a bottle raised in the air as he jammed to the latest Rick Ross hit. But that wasn't what pissed me off. What sent my blood boiling was that while he stood there rocking back and forth, waving his bottle, a girl was grinding up and down him like some desperate hood rat. It made me want to go snatch them both up. I moved through the crowd on the dance floor, and if I thought I couldn't get any more shocked, I did when I saw that the girl who was grinding was none other than Nelly.

"Excuse me," I said loud enough to get J.'s attention.

Nelly did a slow wiggle as she spun around. "What's up, Maya?" she said.

"Uh, you want to tell me what's going on?" I said, ignoring her and turning to J. Love.

"Just chillin'—dancing, having a great time."

"Really? You really got this chick grinding up on you?"

"We're just dancing. Chill out," she said.

I put my hand up. Nobody was talking to her thirsty behind. All I knew was Nelly was really trying to take me there. And yeah, Tamara really needed to see that. Because I was sure that was just what the *Rumor Central* brand needed.

Nelly stopped dancing and stared at me. "Maya, why are you getting all worked up? We're a team now, we share everything," she said, moving in closer to J. Love.

Do you know this dude laughed like that was funny? But the glare in my eyes actually wiped the smile right off his face. Nelly better be glad I wasn't a fighting type of chick because I would've mopped the floor with her silly behind. All I did was spin around and head toward the door.

"Maya, wait up," J. Love said, taking off after me.

"Oh my God, J. Love!" someone screamed, stopping him.

"Hey, babe," he told her, pulling his arm out of her grasp. "I gotta holla at my girl real quick."

"What your girl won't do, I will!" she called out after him.

"Ugh!" I rolled my eyes and kept stomping toward the door.

"Will you chill out?" he said, pulling me to the side once we were in the parking lot. "We were just dancing. You don't want to dance. You just want to sit over there being mad. I'm trying to have a good time. I'm here to support my boy. I've been working my butt off and I just want to party."

"And it looks like you're doing a doggone good job of it."

"Why you trippin' on Nelly? I don't want that girl."

"I can't tell, the way you were letting her grind on you."

He actually smiled again. "It looks like somebody's jealous."

I pushed his shoulder. "This isn't a joke, J. Love. That's disrespectful."

"I wasn't grinding on her, she was grinding on me." He said that like that mess would make all the difference.

"Whatever," I said.

"Babe." He took a step toward me. "Don't be like that."
He actually reached out to hug me. I was tired of being mad
so I decided to let him grovel for a minute.

"How can I make it up to you?" he said.

I was just about to smile when some bold stank-head
chick stepped right up to us, ignored me, and said, "J. Love,
I'm your biggest fan. Can I have your autograph?"

And this hoochie mama opened up her shirt, revealing
silicone fake boobs for him to sign. He looked stunned at
first.

"Please don't make me beg," she purred. "I have a pen
right here." She held up a Sharpie. When he got ready to
reach for it, I couldn't help it. As hard as I could, I pushed him
and turned and stormed over to my car.

Chapter 29

Nothing like some good friends to help you when you're having a bad day. And Kennedi and Sheridan were definitely delivering. They'd had me cracking up, talking about Nelly and her sidekick, Alvin, and J. Love.

"Girl, you need to give that buster a piece of your mind," Kennedi said.

"Oh, now, he's a buster." I laughed. She'd just finished going off about the way J. Love had acted at the party.

We all stopped laughing at the commotion coming from the commons area outside of the cafeteria.

"What's going on out there?" I said, peering at the crowd of people gathered outside.

"I don't know," Sheridan and Kennedi said at the same time.

We made our way through the crowd, and I almost fell over when I saw my *Rumor Central* producer, Dexter, standing off to the side, with a clipboard in hand like he was working. I frowned as I watched him lean over to some guy in a backward baseball cap and whisper something. The guy then began shouting orders to a cameraman. I directed my attention to where the camera lens was aimed and my mouth dropped open at the sight of Nelly Fulton, laughing and talking to Karrington.

"What in the world is going on?" I mumbled, as the camera moved in toward them.

"I have no idea," Sheridan replied.

"Hey, what's going on?" Kennedi asked some girl standing next to her.

The girl smiled proudly. "Oh, they're filming a special on Nelly Fulton."

"For what?" Sheridan asked.

"And who is they?" I added.

The girl shrugged like she didn't know any more than what she'd told us. I knew where I could find out what was going on. I stomped right over to Dexter.

"Excuse me," I said, tapping Dexter on the shoulder.

He spun around and didn't look at all surprised to see me. In fact, he looked irritated.

"What's up, Maya?"

I raised an eyebrow. "You tell me."

"Oh, we're just shooting this special, and these idiot kids keep jumping in the shot." He growled in the direction of my classmate Jock and his band of silly friends.

"I see you're shooting something, but what is it?" I asked.

He sighed. "Look, Maya. I don't have time to do this with you. I'm way over time, which means I'm over budget, which means I'm gonna get my butt chewed out. So you need to call Tamara and have your little temper tantrum with her."

I was speechless. And mad, especially since several of my classmates had witnessed the whole exchange.

"Oh, you'd better believe I'm calling Tamara, and you will be dealt with as well," I snapped.

He gave me the hand. "Girl, bye."

"Ugh," I huffed off. I barely could get my phone out of my purse as I scrambled to call Tamara.

"Good afternoon, this is Tamar—"

I cut Kelley off before she could finish her sentence. "Is Tamara in?"

"May I tell her who's calling?"

"Kelley, you know this is Maya Morgan. I need to speak with Tamara."

I could hear her draw in a breath. "Please hold."

I tapped my feet as I impatiently waited. It felt like an extra long time. I knew Tamara was doing that to irritate me.

"Yes, Maya?"

"Hello, Tamara," I said, deciding to take a sweet approach. "How are you today?"

"Busy. What can I help you with?"

"Hey, umm, just wondering what was going on since the *Rumor Central* crew was up here at my school. Did I miss a memo or something?"

"Actually, it's not the *Rumor Central* crew. Dexter is producing a special on Nelly."

"And why are you doing a special on Nelly?"

"Because *X Factor* is doing a special on her, so we're doing a special on them doing the special."

I rolled my eyes. "And nobody thought I should be involved in that?"

"And why would you be? It's not a *Rumor Central* project."

I was quiet for a moment, then said, "Tamara, I'm not feeling the love at all."

"And, Maya, I'm not feeling your theatrics."

"Excuse me."

"You know, when you're on top, you have a lot more room to make demands. But in case you haven't noticed, *Rumor Central* ratings are down. Your popularity is sinking."

I couldn't believe this. It's like nothing could please these people.

"I'm with J. Love now. What else do you want?"

"You chose love over fame. And it hurt you. Bottom line."

"I'm with him now!"

Tamara sighed, then said, "Let me read you what landed on my desk this morning. The latest issue of *US Weekly*. 'If there's an It Girl in Miami, that title belongs to Nelly Fulton. She's definitely a rising star. With eye candy on her arm, millions of fans, and an unmatchable personality, she is poised to be the next teen queen.' "

"What?"

"No, let me finish," Tamara continued reading. " 'As for Maya Morgan, the beauty formerly known as Diva, she needs to graduate high school, maybe get married and go live in suburbia with her white picket fence.' White picket fence, Maya? Who do you think envies white picket fences? Do you think that's the image we're trying to go for?"

So Bali and those guys were right! Nelly did feed them a story bashing me? I really couldn't believe this.

"So all of this behind who I date. Really?"

"Maya, I'm not going to debate this with you. You know I'm a numbers girl and the numbers right now aren't in your favor."

"This was a setup, Tamara. Nelly was behind this article."

"I don't care who was behind it. It's in print. People are reading it. You're lucky to even still have a job."

"What is that supposed to mean?" I balked.

"It means what it means. Now, I have a ton of work to do. The station manager is in town and I have to explain to him why we're still struggling in the ratings. So, if you'll excuse me, I have to go."

I stood with the phone still to my ear. I knew things were bad. I had no idea they were this bad. I finally hung the phone up and I glanced back over my shoulder. My mouth dropped open as I saw Nelly prance over to Kennedi and

Sheridan. She gave them what looked like a fake laugh, hugged them, then walked off with the camera following.

"Seriously?" I said, approaching them.

"Look, she came over to us," Kennedi said.

"Yeah, we told her we weren't trying to be filmed, but she'd laughed it up for the camera anyway."

I cut my eyes in Nelly's direction. She'd done that to get under my skin. Maybe I had underestimated this girl. Nelly Fulton was definitely trying to play me and I was getting sick and tired of her. In fact, I was getting sick and tired of this whole *Rumor Central* life. It was time to put up or shut up.

Chapter 30

I hadn't told a soul what I was about to do. Not even my BFFs. I didn't need anyone trying to talk me out of it. But a long time ago, I saw an interview from one of my favorite actresses, who left a top-rated TV show. She said if she was going to go out, she was going to go out on top—on her terms. That's exactly what I was about to do.

"Hey, Maya, we made a last-minute change to the script. Nelly's going to read first, then you'll pick up from there." Dexter appeared in my doorway, looking like he was preparing himself for my wrath. The fact that he was here telling me about the script change and not one of his flunkies was proof he was anticipating me going off. But I simply nodded and said, "Okay, got it."

"Okay?" he asked, a bewildered look across his face. "I hope you understand that we're just trying to vary it up," he added, like he felt the need to justify the change.

"I said okay," I repeated.

"Okay," he nervously repeated. "Well, they need you on set."

"I'm heading out," I told him with a smile. As soon as he left, I took a look at my reflection and assured myself that I was doing the right thing.

I made my way onto the set, where hair and makeup immediately went to work, putting touchups on me.

"Hi, Maya," Nelly said.

"Hey," I coldly replied. There wasn't that much faking in the world.

"I hope we're cool with what happened at the party. I was just flirting and playing around."

"Yeah, flirting and playing around with my guy."

"You know I'm with Ross," she felt the need to remind me. "It's not even like that."

"Whatever, Nelly. I can't tell you're with anyone, the way you were grinding over my guy," I said, flipping through and reading over my scripts.

"You can tell you're an only child. You don't like to share anything," she joked.

I rolled my eyes at her just as the director gave me the cue. "All right, ladies, stand by and three, two . . ." He pointed for us to go and Nelly started talking.

"What's up, everybody? It's your girl Nelly Fulton and I'm here with my *cohost*," she said, making sure to put emphasis on the word. I know she was trying to get some type of reaction from me, but I wasn't about to give it to her.

We made it through the show, me using the style and pizzazz I always do. I didn't let all the shade she was throwing knock me off my game. I knew that both Dexter and Tamara were shocked by my reaction because I saw them in the control room looking confused.

"Well, that's it for this edition of *Rumor Central*," Nelly said, wrapping the show up, and turning for me to deliver my closing line.

"We're so glad you tuned in," I continued. "Especially because this will be my last show." I heard the whole room gasp. "That's right. Your girl is out."

Out of the corner of my eye, I saw Tamara and Dexter

going ballistic. I knew I needed to talk fast before they pulled the plug on the camera and sent everything to black.

"The way they do people here at *Rumor Central* is wrong on so many levels. They've encouraged me to stab my friends in the back, dig up dirt on loved ones, and just become an all-around dirty person in the name of ratings. I gave my time and effort to this place and it's never good enough. So, peace and love to you. Your girl Maya Morgan is out. I'll see you when I see you."

I removed my microphone and walked off the set, ignoring the stunned looks on Nelly and the crew's faces. I didn't even know if all of that would make it on air or if they had gone to black in the middle of my good-bye. I didn't care. I was through and I was walking away proudly.

"Have you lost your mind?" Tamara screamed, meeting me in the hallway.

"Nope. In fact, I found it." I didn't back down.

"Maya, what was that?" Dexter said, appearing on the side of her.

"That was me, showing you that I'm done. You guys want to be lowdown with me? Two can play that game. You want Nelly? She's all yours. All by herself."

"I hope you know what you've done," Tamara said. If she was a cartoon, smoke would be coming from her ears.

"Oh, I know all too well," I replied. "So, sue me."

"Trust me, we will," Tamara hissed.

I brushed past them and went into my office. My stuff was already packed and I would send someone to get it. I grabbed my purse and couldn't wait to get out of there. Especially because I didn't want security coming to try and throw me out. I'm not going to lie though, a part of me wished that they would meet me at the door, beg me to stay. But I knew Tamara was furious. It would be a couple of days before she came around. And if she didn't, oh well. I would just have to take my time—and talents—somewhere else.

Chapter 31

"You did what?"

The look on J. Love's face proved exactly why I hadn't told anyone my decision prior to doing it.

We were sitting in the living room of his Miami Beach condo. I'd wanted to tell him what happened once I got here because I wanted to do it in person. I figured he would be shocked. I didn't expect him to be angry.

"I quit. I told you I'm done. If they wanted Nelly to be my cohost then Nelly can host the whole dang thing by herself."

"Really, Maya? You can't share the limelight?" he snapped.

"Oh, okay, so why don't you do your next tour with Chris Brown?" I said, knowing that would shut him up. "Exactly," I continued when he didn't say anything. "You're the star—you don't need to be on stage with another star."

"I'm just saying," he said, pacing back across the room. "That's your claim to fame."

"Fine, I'll find a new claim," I said.

He kept shaking his head like he couldn't believe it. "I just don't think that's the smartest thing you've ever done."

"Well, I'm glad you don't get paid to think for me."

"Whatever."

I couldn't believe the way he was acting. You would've thought he was my manager or something.

"Yeah, whatever, J. Love, just leave it alone." My stomach growled, reminding me that when I'd first arrived thirty minutes ago, he said we would go get something to eat. "Are we going to get something to eat?"

"Naw, I'm not hungry."

"Okay, what's *really* going on?" I said. "That's the whole reason I came over here." Well, that and to explain the whole quitting on air.

"Nothing is going on." He plopped down on his over-sized chair. "I mean it's your life. If you want to throw it away, that's on you."

"I'm not throwing my life away," I said.

He ignored me as he grabbed the remote and flipped the TV on.

I moved and stood in front of the TV, blocking his view. "So were you only with me because I was hosting *Rumor Central*?"

"Don't be ridiculous," he said.

"Well, I can't tell."

"Look, I need to review this video."

That made me smile. "I'm looking forward to the video coming out," I said, hoping if we changed the subject, we could stop fighting.

"Yeah, although we have to revamp some things for that because all the press material says you're the host of *Rumor Central*," he said with a scowl.

That definitely made me side-eye him. He was seriously tripping. I know he liked the whole star couple thing, but he was acting like that's all he liked about me.

He stood, grabbed his cell, and said, "I need to make some calls."

I decided to just let him cool off so for the next hour, I

hung out in J.'s game room while he spent the majority of the time on the phone. He had nothing in his refrigerator so I still hadn't eaten. To say I was livid was an understatement. Finally, I'd had enough.

I made my way downstairs and back to his bedroom to tell him I was leaving. I was just about to call out his name when something stopped me. I eased down the hall because I could hear him on the phone and he sounded upset.

"So, man, I don't know what I'm going to do. She just messed everything up. I know, I know. How she just gonna quit that show like that?"

That made my eyebrows rise.

"I can't replace her. The video is done. But Hype may be able to find someone else for the movie."

Replace me? I thought. Oh, he had lost his mind. I pushed the door open so he could see me. He turned at the sound of the door creaking and his eyes grew wide.

"Say, man, let me call you back." He hung up the phone and immediately started stammering. "M-Maya. Hey, I don't know what you heard."

"Oh, I heard enough," I said. "So now I need to be replaced because I quit my job?"

"Girl, stop trippin'," he said.

"I'm not understanding what's the big deal. Why are you so concerned about *my* job?"

He stepped a little closer to me and tried to wrap his arms around my waist. I pushed him away and stepped back.

"I'm concerned about you," he said. "I know how much you love that job and how much it means to you, and I don't think quitting was the right choice. You know, in this business, it's all about our star power."

"Well, it's done now," I said, tired of arguing. "And I'm sorry if you have a problem with it, but this is my life."

He shrugged. "Okay. Whatever."

More and more lately, I found myself thinking of Alvin. My mind kept drifting back to him. This conversation would've gone so differently if it had been with him. He would've supported my decision, even probably made me feel better about it. I shook that thought away. I couldn't run to Alvin anymore. I'd let him go. Now if only I could let him go from my heart.

Chapter 32

I don't think I'd ever been so excited to see someone in my life. But watching Alvin standing at my door made me want to just throw my arms around his neck.

"Hey, you!" I said with a smile. When I'd seen Alvin at my gate, I had been thrilled and quickly buzzed him in. He'd finally come to his senses and I hoped that we could somehow fix the friction between us. Because this whole thing with J. Love wasn't cutting it. I'd finally left his place last night after he kept acting funky with me.

"Hi, Maya," Alvin said. "Mind if I come in?"

"Of course." I stepped aside to let him in. "You want anything?" I asked, closing the door. "Sui just cleaned up, but she made a fabulous cheesecake that you just have to taste."

Alvin turned around to face me and the look on his face told me he hadn't come here to chitchat.

"No, thank you, Maya. Oh, I'm sorry to hear about you leaving *Rumor Central.* I know how much that show meant to you."

Just the fact that he was sympathetic about that and J. wasn't made me want to cry.

"Thank you. I'll be okay."

"Well, I didn't want to take up too much of your time. I just wanted to talk to you real quick," he continued.

"Cool," I replied. "I want to talk to you, too. I have so much I want to say to you. I just wanted to say, I know things were kinda messed up between us and I know we ended on a bad note, but I really miss you, I mean, I miss your friendship. I miss the way you make me laugh, and I just wish—"

"I'm leaving, Maya," he said, cutting me off.

His words almost knocked me off my feet. "What?"

He took a deep breath. "I'm leaving."

I cocked my head. "Well, when are you coming back?"

"I'm not."

It felt like someone had taken a sledgehammer and slammed it into my stomach. "Wh-what do you mean? You're moving?"

"I'm going to Seattle. Microsoft made me an offer I can't refuse."

I couldn't even form a sentence correctly. "Umm, why? I mean, you, like, I didn't know you were looking for a job. I mean, why can't you work from here?"

"Because the job is in Seattle."

"But you don't need that job. I mean, you have plenty of money."

"You know I don't do what I do for the money."

I was literally shaking. "What about your mother?"

"Mom will be fine. My cousin will move in with her."

"You have this all worked out."

"Yeah, it just came all of a sudden. I mean, they interviewed me and offered me the job in a matter of two weeks."

"Two weeks? Why are you just now telling me?"

He looked at me crazy. "Why would I have told you? We're not together."

"But we—I mean . . ." I didn't even know what to say. I'm sure I sounded like a bumbling idiot.

"Look, Maya. You're all over the blogs, in magazines.

J. Love got what he wanted. You. You made your choice and I was trying to respect your decision."

I wanted to cry and tell him that I'd made a bad choice. A dumb choice.

"The only reason I'm here now," he continued, "is because we did used to be friends."

We were more than friends. I love you! I wanted to shout. But I didn't open my mouth because if I did, I just knew I would burst out crying.

"Why do you need to go?" I finally said.

"Why do I need to stay?"

Me! Stay for me! I wanted to shout. But staring in Alvin's eyes, I knew I had no right, so I didn't say anything.

After a few minutes, Alvin said, "Well, I just came by to tell you that."

"When do you leave?"

"In two weeks."

It felt like my world was falling in, and I had no idea what to do about it.

"So, you'll miss my graduation?"

He shifted from one foot to another.

"Yeah. I probably won't be able to make it back," he replied.

I didn't think it was possible for me to be any more hurt, but that was a slap in the face.

"Yeah, Seattle is pretty far," he added.

"That's what airplanes are for."

He stared at me. I couldn't be sure, but it seemed like his eyes were watering up as well. "It's probably not a good idea anyway."

"So, it's like that now?" I said, trying to keep my voice from cracking.

He nodded, but didn't respond. Finally, I said, "All right, cool. I see what our relationship meant to you."

"Don't do that, Maya, because you know why—"

"Nah, nah. It's all good," I said, holding my hands up. "You go on to Seattle. Start your new life. I'm good." I was trying to display a hardness I didn't really feel.

"Maya . . ."

I turned and headed toward my stairs. "See yourself out."

"Maya . . ."

I kept walking, ignoring his pleas for me to hear him out. I didn't stop as I headed up the stairs. I couldn't stop. Because if I did, I would collapse to the floor in tears.

Chapter 33

I should be excited. *Should be.*

I'd gotten the good news—my contract for the film was signed, sealed, and delivered. J. Love and I had made up, or at least stopped fighting. So why wasn't I happy?

The world premiere of the video with J. Love was in two days. And me and J. had a round of interviews. I really didn't want to do them, but that stupid contract I'd signed required me to do media to promote the video, so I had to. And I was already waiting to see if I was getting in trouble behind my quitting *Rumor Central*.

"So, Maya, how do you feel about branching out?" the television host asked.

"I'm sorry?" I replied, snapping my attention back to her. We were on the set of *Behind the Scenes*, an entertainment show that talked about upcoming videos.

J. Love huffed his agitation. We'd argued every day since I left his house, about everything.

"Are you here with me today?" the host laughed.

I wanted to tell her no. While I was excited about the video, and even the movie, my mind was on how jacked up my life had become. I couldn't put my finger on why I was so bummed out. It couldn't be because I'd left *Rumor Central*. I'd made that decision, and the fact that no one had called to come after me, good or bad, didn't seem to faze me. Yes, a part of me was disappointed that they were willing to let me go, but I just took that to mean that it was time for me to go. I refused to believe that it was because of Alvin.

"Hello."

"Yes, umm, yes," I replied.

J. Love stepped in. "We're very excited for this project. It's been fast-tracked and we're just happy Maya stepped up at the last minute. Hype Lee did an amazing job."

"Well, we're excited about it, too. And we just love seeing you two together. So, tell me, do you still feel she's perfect for you?" the woman asked with a sly smile.

I expected him to say "Absolutely" or something else like that, but he just gave the woman a stupid smile and didn't respond.

"Well, is there trouble in paradise?" she said, being messy.

"We're here to focus on the movie, that's it," J. Love said.

I tried my best not to side-eye him the rest of the interview, but afterward, I couldn't wait until we were back in the car.

"What was that about?" I asked him.

"You tell me," he said, leaning in and turning on the radio in his Hummer. "You the one acting like you didn't want to be there."

"I just have a lot on my mind, J. You know I'm going through some stuff."

"Whatever. Where do you want me to drop you?"

I just stared at him.

"Where?" he repeated. "Home or w—well, I guess I can't say work, since you don't work."

I turned back around in my seat. "Oh, you're for-real trippin'."

He didn't say another word as he turned the music up and blared it all the way to my house.

I got out in front of my house without saying a word to J. I couldn't for the life of me understand why he had an attitude with me. So my mind wasn't completely in the interview? That wasn't a reason for him to be a complete prick.

I had just made my way inside and walked over to the refrigerator to find something to eat when my phone rang. I didn't recognize the number, but I went ahead and answered. "Hello."

"Hi, Maya." I rolled my eyes, closed the refrigerator, and walked over and plopped down at the kitchen table. I was not in the mood for Nelly Fulton.

"What do you want?" I said.

"See, that's that mess I'm talking about," Nelly said. The chipperness was gone from her voice and she sounded like she had an attitude. "All I have done is try to be your friend. I'm sorry you were so threatened by me that you had to quit *Rumor Central*."

"Girl, please," I said. "Nobody is threatened by your whack behind."

"Tell yourself that if it makes you feel better." She exhaled. "Look, I wasn't calling you to fight. I was trying to see if you wouldn't mind turning over some of your contacts to me since I don't know a lot of people in Miami."

I had to pull the phone away from my ear and stare at it. Was this girl for real? I even looked around my kitchen. Surely, I was being punked.

"I mean, you can't do anything with them anymore. So, I was hoping you would just give them to me," she continued.

"Nelly, I don't know what kind of supersonic drugs you are on, but you have lost your mind."

"Maya, you don't want to make an enemy of me. I am the new host of *Rumor Central* and I really can make your life miserable."

I swear I would've been furious if this wasn't so funny. "Nelly. I'm really not in the mood for this craziness you're talking on my phone. I wish I would give you an initial of one of my contacts. You wanted the job, it's yours. Now make it work."

She was silent for a minute. Then, she said, "Fine. I will. And guess who's going to be the target of my first story? You. I know you have some dirt in your closet somewhere and I'm going to find it. Bet on that."

"Do you, Nelly. Do you." I hung the phone up. Programmed her number in my phone as NutBasket, then tossed my phone on the counter.

Everybody was losing their minds.

Chapter 34

I missed my man. It wasn't just because J. Love had turned out to be a total jerk, but I really and truly missed Alvin—his corny ways, his attentiveness, even those Coke-bottle glasses. It was true that you never really knew what you had until it was gone.

I laid across my bed, twirling my phone in my hand, wondering if I should call Alvin. Only I didn't know what to say. Maya Morgan didn't beg, but I wanted to say anything to get my boo back. Before I could make up my mind, my phone rang. I smiled when I saw my cousin Travis's name pop up on the screen.

"I can't believe you're actually calling and not texting," I said, answering.

"What's up, girl?" he said. "I do know how to use the phone. I just know you busy leading that superstar life, so texting is easier. What you up to?"

I could picture him multitasking (playing video games, cleaning his tennis shoes) because he never sat still and just did one thing. "Same ol' same ol'," I replied.

"Then that means you're still pissing people off." He laughed.

"You still getting in trouble?" I shot back. The whole reason Travis had come to live with us in the first place was because he'd gotten into trouble from hanging around the wrong crowd and skipping school. Aunt Bev, my dad's sister, was a single parent who had already lost one son to gang violence. She wasn't about to lose another, so she'd sent him to live with us.

"Nah, trying to stay out of trouble," Travis said. "I can't be stressin' Mama out any more than I already have."

"How's Aunt Bev?"

"Better. The doctors had all but given up, but she went to a different specialist and it looks like stuff is turning around. I'm glad Uncle Myles could help."

"I just can't believe you didn't tell us in the first place. You know Daddy would've helped."

"You know my mama is stubborn." Travis laughed. "Well, I saw you and your boy all over the blogs. I thought you was giving Alvin a chance."

I blew a frustrated breath. "I was. I mean, me and Alvin were together. But he broke up with me," I said, finally admitting it to someone.

"What?"

"Yeah. He said he couldn't take the celebrity life anymore."

"Wow. When I saw J. Love on MTV talking about he was going to make you his, I thought he was just mouthing off. I didn't think he really would do it."

I always get what I want. J. Love's words popped into my head at that moment and I actually felt stupid.

"Yeah, I don't even know how I ended up back with J. I haven't told anyone this, but I regret losing Alvin, I really do."

"Dang, cuz, I hate to hear that."

"Alvin is moving," I said, actually trying to keep my voice from cracking.

"Um, are you about to cry?" Travis asked.

I swallowed hard, and before I knew it, the tears were falling down my cheeks. I sat up on my bed and buried my face in my hands. "I messed up, Travis. I want him back." I was shocking myself. Never in a katrillion years did I think I'd be sitting up boo-hooing over some dude like this.

I guess Travis couldn't believe it either because he said, "Wow. I never thought I'd see the day that my cousin, THE Maya Morgan, would shed tears over a dude."

"I know, right," I said, managing a faint chuckle as I wiped my tears.

"That must mean that he's pretty special and you need to let him know that."

"But he's leaving."

"And? I mean, he hasn't left yet so it's not too late. Have you told him how you feel?"

"No."

"Then that's where you need to start. I know that you're super diva and all, but you're also human. Call the boy. Tell him that you made a mistake and you want to make it right."

I was quiet as I thought about what Travis was saying. "You're right," I finally said.

"I'm always right," he replied.

We made small talk for a few more minutes, then made promises to do a better job of keeping in touch, before hanging up. I took a few deep breaths, then dialed Alvin's number. Just when I thought it was going to go to voice mail, the phone picked up.

"Hello."

I paused at the sound of the female voice. "Ah, is, uh . . ."

"Yes, Maya?" she said and I instantly recognized Marisol's voice. What was she doing answering Alvin's phone? "Do you want Alvin? Because he can't come to the phone right now. He's packing *our* stuff."

"Our?" I said, without even realizing it.

"Oh, yes. Our. We're moving to Seattle."

"We?" How was that even possible? I thought she'd be under somebody's jail. How could she be getting ready to move? And with my man.

"That's right, we. Alvin paid for a top notch attorney for me, so they're working everything out now." She sighed like I was an annoying fly or something. "Look, Alvin had his little phase with you, but then he came back to the one he really loves. He's forgiven me for what I did and we're moving forward."

That made me pause. She had to be lying. There was no way Alvin would get back with Marisol. Would he?

"Girl, whatever. Put Alvin on the phone," I said, fuming that Alvin even had her up in his house.

"I guess you think I'm playing," Marisol snapped. "I'm in his house. I'm answering his phone and I'm helping him realize that you are only about that celeb life. He told me all about you and J. Love. And when he told you he was fed up, he meant it. So you enjoy your celeb-filled life, and me and my man will enjoy ours. Don't call him again. Got it?"

She hung up the phone in my face and I was too stunned to be furious. My first thought was that she was lying, but if he'd told her about J. Love, and she was at his house, answering his phone, maybe he had gotten back with her. I couldn't believe it. And she was moving with him? I was sitting here shedding tears over this guy and he'd already moved on— with her of all people? I didn't think it was possible, but I felt even more hurt than I had before.

Chapter 35

It felt funny sitting at home watching my show live. I shook away that thought. *Rumor Central* was no longer my show. I needed to get that out of my head.

I heard the back door open and the clink of my father's keys as he tossed them on the bar. I knew it wasn't my mother because she was off getting some kind of eight-hour spa treatment. Besides, when I was a little girl, I used to wait for the clink of those keys to let me know my daddy was home.

"Hey, Daddy," I said as he walked into the den.

"How's my sweet pea today?"

"Not good." I turned my attention away from the TV and back to the email I'd printed out from our family attorney. Just when I'd thought my week couldn't get any worse, I got this email that WXIA was moving forward with plans to sue me for quitting and violating my *Rumor Central* contract. "Can you handle this? I can't deal with this stuff," I said, handing him the email.

"What's wrong?" he asked, taking the paper.

"The station said they're going to sue me," I said.

"Oh, that." He waved me off as he set the paper down. "Walter called me about that."

"You don't seem fazed," I replied. I'd been sitting here stressing for the past hour, and my dad was acting like it was a summons for jury duty.

"Darling, if I had a dime for every time someone threatened to sue me, we'd be even richer than we are."

I smiled at my dad. I loved how it took a lot to make him sweat. The only time I'd seen him nervous was when a former partner had gotten caught up in some illegal activity and my dad was worried that his name would be tied to it. But as usual, my dad had come out on top.

"How do you know they're not really going to sue?" I asked.

My dad smiled. "Let's just say that whole dangerous trip to Cancún they sent you on left them wide open."

"What do you mean?" For spring break, we had taken a senior trip to Cancún that the station all but forced me to film. They were hoping I could get some dirt since a lot of young celebrities went to the Spring Break Fling. That's when Evian had faked her kidnapping after going off with some guy during a game of truth-or-dare. We'd gone crazy trying to find her and had gone to some pretty shady places, but nothing had happened to us, so I didn't know what that whole trip had to do with anything.

"You're seventeen, sweetheart," my dad explained. "The station placed you in a position that could've ended very badly in pursuit of a story. So, we reminded them that, as soon as their lawsuit was filed, we would be pressing charges for endangering the welfare of a minor."

I frowned in confusion. "But I agreed to do that."

"By the time we got through in court, you'd be a young, naïve, starstruck girl who was coerced into putting her life in danger for the sake of ratings."

I couldn't do anything but smile. My dad could be ruthless. I guess he wasn't a multimillionaire businessman for
nothing. "So you think they bought it?" I asked.

"Oh, they have to take it back to the bigwigs, but I doubt
they want to mess with a Morgan child," he said, squeezing
my cheek. But then his voice turned serious. "I want you to
take some time off and enjoy the rest of your senior year and
the summer."

"I'm trying."

"You have the rest of your life to be an adult and live a
lavish life. Enjoy your youth. And since you start college in
the fall, you especially need to just relax."

I couldn't respond to that because it wasn't written I was
going to college. I mean, people went to college so they
could get good jobs. I had a good job. *Or I used to*, the little
voice in my head said. Regardless, I definitely wasn't about
to get into that with my dad, so I just nodded and said,
"Thanks, Dad."

He leaned in and kissed me on the forehead. "Of course.
You don't worry your pretty little head about this nonsense.
Walter and I have it handled. Can you tell Sui I'm going to
take dinner in my office tonight?"

I pulled out my phone and started browsing Instagram
when I saw a text come in.

To all my friends, just want to say I'll miss you guys. KIT

I frowned when I noticed it was from Alvin. I opened the
message. He had sent it to me and seven other people. The
guy that I loved had really and truly sent me a good-bye note
via a group text? I didn't know whether to be mad or hurt.
And now, knowing that Marisol was moving to Seattle with
Alvin, I couldn't help but wonder if I had ever really meant
anything to Alvin at all.

Chapter 36

I couldn't believe I was sitting outside Alvin's house, ducked down in Sui's car, watching him load his U-Haul. What in the world had I turned into? Divas didn't do this. But I couldn't let him leave without saying something. I just had to figure out what.

I'd tossed and turned all night. His group text had really disturbed me and I'd thought about calling him to go off, but I needed to do this face-to-face.

I didn't see Marisol anywhere around, and believe me, I was looking, because the last thing I wanted was her to have the satisfaction of seeing me grovel.

I took a deep breath to give me strength, then pulled up behind the U-Haul. Alvin was walking out with a box. He stopped when he saw me and didn't say a word as I slowly got out of the car and walked toward him.

"Hey," I said.

"Hey," he replied.

"So, you're all packed?"

"Yeah," he said, walking around me and placing the box on the back of the truck.

"What about your mom? Are you really going to leave your mom?" I asked, just because I didn't have the courage to say what I really wanted to say yet.

"My mom is straight. My cousin is going to come move in here. She was all too happy to have a free place to live, so Mom will be taken care of," Alvin replied. "And I'll be back and forth."

That actually brought a smile to my face. Seattle was on the other side of the country, but knowing that this wouldn't be the last time I saw Alvin gave me a little glimmer of hope.

"So, what did you want, Maya?" he asked. I couldn't believe how cold and callous he was.

"I just wanted to say good-bye."

"We did that already."

"Yeah, in a group text. That's what I've been reduced to? A group text?"

He sighed like he didn't want to argue with me.

"How could you take her with you?" I finally blurted out. "You swore that nothing was going on." With anyone else, I would've never let myself appear so desperate, but there was something about Alvin. I didn't mind showing my vulnerability.

"What are you talking about, Maya?"

"Marisol. When the picture of you two was in the paper, you said you weren't messing around with her, but something was going on for you to jump back into a relationship with her so fast. I just can't believe you're taking her with you, especially after everything that happened. Do you have any idea how much that hurts?"

He scratched his head in confusion. "What? Who said I was taking her with me?"

"Um, she did."

Alvin actually started laughing. "First of all, Maya, what I said was true. There was nothing going on. Marisol asked me to meet her because she wanted to tell me that she planned to plead guilty to causing your accident. She wanted to apologize to me and say good-bye because she thought she'd be going to jail for a while. She caught me by surprise when she leaned in and kissed me and I told her that was out of order. Secondly, not that it's any of your business, but she's not going to Seattle with me."

"What? But I called you last week and she said she was going with you."

He rolled his eyes and shook his head at the same time. "And you believed her? She came over to get some stuff that had been in my basement that she wanted to leave with her mother before she went away. I didn't know that you had called and I sure didn't know that she had answered my phone. But she was messing with you. She's not going anywhere with me. I'm not involved with her. At all."

That made me want to jump for joy and cry at the same time. "Oh, wow." I moved into him with a smile. He took a step back, which wiped the smile right off of my face.

"I'm not involved with anybody. You, on the other hand, are."

That stung. But I guess I deserved it. "Alvin, I made a mistake. I mean, the whole thing with J. wasn't even like that."

"Whatever, Maya. You wanted somebody to make you look good, go look good."

I didn't know what to say. I actually deserved his anger, and judging from the look in his eyes, boy was he angry.

"Alvin, what do you want me to say?"

"There's nothing else for you to say, Maya. I'm not about that life. Never have been. Never will be. I thought I could make you happy, but I can't change the way I look as much as you'd like me too. And despite your text, I will never be hot."

I looked at him in confusion. "What are you talking about?"

"You really gotta do better with texting the right person.

I saw the text I'm assuming was meant for one of your girls. *If only Alvin was hot.* Well, I'm not."

I was speechless. I remembered Tamara calling me out during that meeting, so I'd quickly pressed SEND, thinking I'd sent the text to Kennedi.

When I didn't say anything, Alvin continued, "Yeah, I don't know who you were trying to text, but it went to me instead."

"A-Alvin, let me explain."

He held up his hand. "It's all good, Maya." He shook his head. "I'm not what you want."

"Yes, you are," I cried.

"No, I'm what you want till some real eye candy comes along. I need someone who wants me for me. So, I'm gonna holla at you later. Take care of yourself and stay out of trouble."

Then he turned and walked back in the house and my heart told me that was the last time I'd ever see Alvin Martin.

Chapter 37

If you can't be with the one you love, love the one you're with.

I remember my grandmother used to play this old blues song that went something like that. When I was little, I'd had no idea what that meant. But now, I think I knew.

I'd lost Alvin, and as much as J. Love got on my nerves, I might as well just kick it with him. I know we'd had our share of problems, but I really didn't feel like starting all over on the dating scene. I'd lost my job; the least I could do was hang on to my guy.

We'd been hanging out at his place all day. I usually didn't like chillin' alone in his crib for too long because he was used to getting any woman he wanted. And I didn't want to put myself in any tempting position. But so far, to my surprise, he didn't press the issue.

"I'm about to take a shower." J. Love walked into the living room, where I'd been sitting and flipping through the latest issue of *Miami Hot Gossip*. "You good?" he asked, even though it seemed like he was just asking to be asking.

"Yeah." I closed the magazine. I'd wasted enough time. I needed to do my homework in case J. wanted to go do something after he got out of the shower. "Can I use your laptop?" I asked him. "I might as well go ahead and look up this stuff I need for the history final paper."

"Yeah, it's on the dining room table." He pointed across the living room. He didn't say anything else, which had sorta become our story. It's like we didn't have as much to say to each other anymore. We didn't have fun. We didn't even really talk, and I had no idea why things had changed. I could tell it was only a matter of time before things fell apart for us altogether.

I opened up the laptop, logged on to Google, and started pulling research. At least if I printed some stuff or at least got the links, I'd have all the info so when I got home I could just pull what I needed.

I had been working for about five minutes when J.'s IM dinged, letting me know he had a message. It was from someone named Cale.

Hey, glad everything worked out n ol' boy is out the picture

That made me frown. *Ol' boy is out the picture.* What did that mean?

I hesitated, then glanced around to make sure J. was still in the shower. I don't know what made me type:

Thanks for helping me make that happen.

I knew J. would have a fit if he knew what I was doing, but something in my gut told me I didn't need to walk away and my gut was usually right on the money.

No prob. When your unc is head of Microsoft, u can make things happen. lol

The nerves in my stomach tightened. I didn't want to say the wrong thing. I slowly typed:

Didn't think u could do it

I didn't know what *it* was, but I was hoping I didn't say too much to give things away.

LOL. Ol boy was more than qualified. Shoot, my unc
said u did him a favor. When he saw dude's resume,
he was pumped

I couldn't breathe. I sat, fuming. This had to be some kind of huge misunderstanding. There had to be someone else that J. Love had helped get a job at Microsoft.

"What are you doing?"

I jumped at the sound of J.'s voice. My first thought was to try and hide the IM, but I was too angry to hide anything and I wanted to know the truth.

"What is this?" I pointed to the laptop screen.

"What are you talking about?" He walked over to me.

I jabbed at the screen again. "This IM."

J. Love leaned in to read it. His eyes grew wide. "You posed as me?"

I ignored his accusation and said, "What is he talking about? *Who* is he talking about?"

J. Love had the nerve to look at me crazy.

"I can't believe that you are all up in my stuff like that."

"I wasn't in your stuff," I said. "It popped up on the screen."

"And you just had to answer pretending to be me?"

I wasn't about to let him turn this around on me. "Did you have something to do with Alvin getting that job in Seattle?"

He rolled his eyes but didn't reply.

"Answer me!"

Finally, he shrugged. "So what if I did?"

"Why would you do that?" I asked, dumbfounded.

He shrugged like it was no big deal. "Look, I was just trying to help a brother out."

"Are you serious?" I screamed.

"First of all, you need to lower your voice," he warned me. "Secondly, don't worry about why I do what I do."

I was speechless. "So, you got him another job in another state to break us up."

"Oh, you were already broken up. I just got him out the way altogether. I told you, I play to win." He had the nerve to smile.

"I am not some stupid chess game!" I screamed.

"I told you, I always get what I want. By any means necessary." He leaned in, closed his laptop, and picked it up.

"What does that mean?"

J. Love smirked like he had a secret he was proud of.

"What? You all big and bad to try and take pride in breaking us up, own up to what you did."

He actually laughed. Then, he shocked me even more when he said, "It might be easier to tell you what I *didn't* do. Those balcony seats." He raised one finger. "One call. That ditzy ex-girlfriend of his, well, she was all too willing to help me. Told her where to be, when to kiss, so the photographer could catch it. Oh, yeah, and I can't forget about the pics when we went out. She made sure he saw those on Instagram too. Should I go on?"

"I don't believe this." I shook my head like I was in the middle of a bad dream.

"Believe it. Everything was all planned by your boy." He pounded his chest.

I had no words, so I just said, "Why?"

"I told you. J. Love always gets what he wants. Plain and simple."

I couldn't believe he was standing here telling me this. But now that I thought about it, that was the arrogance of J. Love. He was actually proud of what he'd done.

"So all of this was a power play?" I asked.

"Girl, we're supposed to be a power couple and you went and messed it all up." He snarled like I had really messed up a master plan.

I was speechless. J. Love had carefully orchestrated all of this.

"But if I had known you were gonna quit your job and become some nagging slob, I wouldn't have bothered," he threw in.

"Nagging slob? You got me messed up." I might have been a little depressed lately and I might not have even been my usual fly self, but I was far from a nagging slob.

He turned up his nose in disgust. "Look at you. The Maya Morgan I met was fabulous. You have on baggy sweats and a tank top."

"These are yoga pants, idiot!"

"Whatever. You are far from the hot star I need to be rolling with. So, quiet as it's kept, why don't you bounce? I've had my fun with you and now I'm through."

I grabbed my purse before I caught a case. "My appearance might have changed," I said, stepping in his face. "But one thing hasn't. I don't let anyone play me. And trust, you messed with the wrong one."

"Girl, bye," he said, putting his hand in my face. "I'm platinum, baby. I need a star on my arm." He motioned up and down my body. "And you are definitely no longer a star."

I paused near the front door. "Oh, don't get it twisted. Whether I'm working for *Rumor Central* or not, whether I'm rocking Versace or a onesie, I'm all that. And you, you fake, wannabe thug, are going to regret that you ever crossed me. You can bet your *platinum* status on that."

I didn't give him time to respond as I walked out the door, slamming it as hard as I possibly could.

Chapter 38

I didn't think it was possible, but I'd calmed down some from yesterday. I'd thought of a hundred ways to get back at J. Love, but ultimately, I'd decided the best revenge would be not to give him a moment more of my time. J. Love would get his. I didn't know how or when, but I was confident that he would.

I pulled out of the Aventura Mall parking lot. I'd come here to clear my mind and just try to get a little retail therapy to make me feel better. Two hours and two thousand and six hundred dollars later, I felt a lot better.

I had just pulled onto the freeway when my phone rang. I looked down to see Yolanda's name on the screen. She'd been sick when she'd learned that I'd just up and quit *Rumor Central*. I think her feelings were also hurt that I'd quit without saying anything to her, but I couldn't let anyone know what I was doing. We'd spoken briefly by phone after that, but hadn't really had a chance to talk in depth. I assumed that's what this call was about.

I pushed the TALK button. "Hey, Yolanda," I said.

"Hi, Maya." Her voice sounded strained. "How are you?"

"Never better," I replied.

"Well, um, hey, I was wondering. I know you're really busy, but do you have time to meet me today?"

She wanted to talk face-to-face. She must've really been upset with me. Normally, I wouldn't have cared, but Yolanda had been a really good assistant and believe me, I'd been the wringer with assistants.

"Yeah. I'm just leaving Aventura Mall. I have a few minutes and can meet you somewhere around here."

"Can you meet me at the Starbucks on the corner by the mall? I won't take up much of your time."

"Okay, but what is it?" I asked.

"I'd just rather do this in person," she said.

Now she really had my interest piqued, because the tone of her voice sounded like more than just *I want to say good-bye.*

"So what's going on?" I asked her twenty minutes later, as I sat across from her at Starbucks. "How are you?"

"I've seen better days," she said. I knew she was a struggling college student. Unlike my past assistants, she'd never seemed to have a problem working for someone younger than her.

I let out a heavy sigh. "Look, I'm sorry. I know that the whole way I left wasn't good, but you have to understand I had to leave and I didn't want to tell anyone what I was doing."

"I understand that," she said. "I mean, I don't like how it all went down, but I understand why you did it. They really charged me up like I knew what you were going to do."

I hadn't even thought about the possibility that they would fire her because she was my assistant.

"That's exactly why I didn't tell you," I said. "Please tell me they didn't fire you."

"No," she said. "Although I don't know how much longer I'm going to be there."

"Look, you don't have to leave because of me."

"No, that's not it," she said. "I'm Nelly's assistant now."

"What?"

"Yeah, they moved me over to her and I don't like her."

I smiled. Yolanda had to be one of the first people to say that. Everybody else was so fooled by her.

"She's so fake."

"Tell me about it," I replied.

"No, seriously, it's like she's one way with them and then she's completely different when she's alone with me. She's real disrespectful and she talks to me really crazy. Then she plays all sweet and innocent when people come around."

That didn't surprise me. But I wondered if that's why Yolanda was here—just to Nelly bash. While I enjoyed hearing it, I really had better things to do.

"So is that what you wanted to talk to me about?"

"Well, kind of." She fidgeted with her purse strap. "There was something else. I know that I shouldn't have done this, and I need to assure you that I never did anything like this with you. I never invaded your personal space."

"Okay," I said, wondering why she was giving me a disclaimer.

She pulled out a piece of paper. "Well, what initially got me going was the station wanted me to pull some background info on Nelly for the feature story that they're doing. So, I started doing some digging. And it was just really strange to me that I couldn't find any information about her prior to going on *X Factor*."

I failed to see where she was going with this. "Well, she was a nobody, a homeless orphan, so maybe that's why there was nothing out there."

"That's what I thought, until I asked her about it. I told her I wanted to get information on her hometown so I could pull up old pictures and get names of people who knew her back then. She went completely ballistic. She told me I'd better say exactly what she told me to say and there was no need for me to go digging for anything. Well, you know that only made me dig more."

I smiled. "I guess I taught you well."

She smiled back. "You did, and Nelly's story doesn't add up."

"What are you talking about?"

"She claims she was an orphan, but it's hard to believe she lived on the streets as a child. It seems like she would've been in somebody's system. But there's *nothing*. It's like she didn't exist." Yolanda slid a piece of paper to me. She hesitated like she really wasn't sure about her next move. "I went on her personal computer and I saw an email from someone who claimed to be her father," Yolanda continued. "It looks like he was trying to strong-arm her for money and threatened to tell her 'little secret.' I traced the IP address and it came from a computer at Chattahoochee High School in Chatta-hoochee, Florida."

"Wow," I said, impressed by all of the info that Yolanda had dug up.

"I don't know anything more. I'm guessing that's where she went to high school? I don't know. I'm just saying I smell something funny and I've hit a dead end. Honestly, I don't even know what to do with this info, but I thought about you and thought maybe there's something you can find out. You're much better at this than me. If I'm being honest, I'd love nothing more than to expose this woman for the fraud I know she is."

I took the piece of paper. Fraud? Oh, Yolanda just didn't know; if there was a chance that Nelly wasn't on the up-and-up, I wouldn't stop digging until I found out for sure.

Chapter 39

There was a reason that I had been on top of my game at *Rumor Central*. I had a sixth sense. My gut told me when something wasn't right, and from the moment I'd met her, I'd definitely felt something wasn't right with Nelly Fulton. Yes, she'd basically stolen my job with *Rumor Central*, but I didn't blame her completely. She'd had an opportunity and gone for it. I couldn't help but respect that. But what I couldn't appreciate was the phony concern. Just take the job and do you. All that calling and trying to play the sympathetic role didn't set right with me. And then, she had the nerve to try and come for me? Even still, I probably should've just walked away, but my instincts wouldn't let me. Especially after everything that Yolanda had told me. Now, my curiosity was more than piqued.

That's why I was on this crop-duster plane about to land in Chattahoochee, Florida. My mom would kill me if she knew that I had caught a flight out without telling anyone. Thankfully, neither she nor my father really checked my credit card bill as long as it wasn't too high. But I had to get to the bottom of this.

I walked through the small security exit. The driver for

the car service I'd hired was standing there with a sign with my name on it.

"Hi, I'm Maya Morgan," I said, approaching him.

"Hello. I'm Rafael White. How was your flight?"

"Fine. Bumpy." This was a little regional airport, and there couldn't have been ten people on my flight.

"You don't have any luggage?" Rafael asked.

"Nah, just here for the day," I replied. "The company did tell you you'd be with me all day?"

"Yes, ma'am. I'm yours all day." He motioned toward the door. "This way."

He led me out to his town car. "So where's the first stop?" he asked once we were both settled in.

"Chattahoochee High School." I didn't know how old Nelly was, but her Wikipedia page put her at nineteen, so that would mean someone still around would remember her.

We made it to the high school just as the kids were getting out.

"Okay, wait right here," I told the driver.

I pulled my hair up into a ponytail and pushed the store-bought reading glasses I'd bought on the way in up on my face. Today was not a day that I wanted to be recognized, which was the only reason I'd dared step out in public with no makeup on.

"Excuse me," I said, stopping a man who looked like a janitor picking up trash. "Where's the front office?"

"Right through those double doors," he said, pointing to my right. "Follow me. I was just heading in."

I followed him to the office and thanked him as he began picking up some papers on the floor there.

There was a flurry of activity behind the counter, including a heavyset woman who was sorting files at the counter. She greeted me with a hearty, "Hello."

"Hi, I'm a reporter for the *Miami Herald* and we're doing a story on Nelly Fulton." I spoke with a high pitch, just in case someone recognized my voice. I was hoping that these old people working the front desk didn't watch *Rumor Central*.

"The *X Factor* winner?" the woman asked, looking confused.

I had come up with the reporter story because I didn't know any other way to get information. Honestly, I didn't even know what I was looking for. I just wanted to see what I could dig up. "Yes, ma'am. We're doing a story on her and I was hoping you could tell me where I could catch up with some of her teachers."

"I suppose wherever she went to school," the woman said, looking at me strangely.

"She didn't go here?" I asked.

"No, she sure didn't. At least not in the past five years that I've been here."

"But I was told that she went here," I said, hoping the woman was mistaken.

"Then you were told wrong." The woman gave me a genuine smile.

"So Nelly Fulton didn't go here?" I asked. I hoped that I hadn't come on a wild goose chase. I'd done some research myself. There was a Margaret Fulton listed in Chattahoochee. When I'd called the number and asked for Nelly, the elderly woman had said she wasn't in, but asked did I want to leave a message. That's why I'd decided to hop a plane and come see what I could find out.

"No, ma'am. I'm sorry," the woman said. "Chattahoochee isn't but so big and I know every student that comes through. And if we had a superstar like Nelly Fulton in our ranks, her picture would be hanging right there." She pointed to the wall behind me.

"But I talked with a Margaret Fulton and she said Nelly wasn't home but she'd take a message, so I just assumed . . ."

The woman laughed. "Mrs. Margaret? Honey, she is just as senile as the day is long! You could've asked for Barack Obama and she would've told you he'd run to the grocery store. But as far as I know, she ain't no kin to Nelly Fulton."

I didn't know what to say. I had just known I'd get some answers here. "Well, I'm sorry to bother you," I told her, trying not to sound defeated.

I had just made my way back outside when the janitor that I'd talked to earlier approached me.

"Excuse me," he said. "I couldn't help but overhear. You a reporter looking for information about Nelly Fulton?"

I nodded. "I thought she went to this school."

He looked at me for a moment, then leaned in and said with a smile, "She didn't. But Nadra Franklin did."

"What? Who is Nadra Franklin?"

He looked around nervously. "How much y'all paying for that information?"

"Well, if you have some good information, I'll make it worth your while."

He continued fidgeting. "Well, I can't do this here. Where are you staying? Maybe I can come to your hotel."

He must've thought I was crazy. I didn't know if he was legit or not, but I wasn't about to be alone with him to find out. "Maybe there's a Starbucks around that we can meet at," I told him.

He laughed. "You're definitely big city. The nearest Starbucks is about fifty-two miles away. But we can meet at the McDonald's."

I cringed at the thought. I hadn't set foot in a McDonald's since I was four. But I'd do what I needed to do to get to the truth.

"Okay, fine. Which one?"

"The only one in town. On Main Street. I get off in an hour. I'll meet you there."

"Okay, my friend will bring me." I just wanted to let this guy know I wouldn't be alone in case he turned out to be a creep.

But he just said, "Okay, see you then." Then he scurried off.

"So what do you want to do?" the driver asked when I got back in the car.

I had an hour to kill, so I said, "I'd like to find a library." I was thinking maybe I could look in the town's archives and find some old newspaper clippings. I'd Googled Nelly before I'd come, but I'd gotten nothing but a bunch of stuff that came after her *X Factor* win. Yolanda was right. It was almost as if she hadn't existed before the show.

Ten minutes later, I was sitting in front of an outdated computer, going through old Chattahoochee newspaper clippings. There was no mention of Nelly Fulton anywhere locally, which was strange because the girl had won *X Factor*. You'd think they would have it plastered all over the place.

She didn't go here, but Nadra Franklin did.

The janitor's words popped into my head. That's when it dawned on me that it wasn't unusual for people in show business to change their names. Everyone couldn't have a fabulous showbiz-ready name like Maya Morgan.

I went back to the search box and typed in *Nadra Franklin*. Nothing came up except a 1995 article about a sixth-grade girl by that name winning the local spelling bee.

I sighed, then noticed the time. It had been almost forty-five minutes, so I logged off and made my way back out to the car. Rafael had dozed off, so I tapped the window. He jumped, then scurried out of the car.

"I'm so sorry," he muttered, opening my door.

"It's okay. We're going to head to that McDonald's we passed on the way in."

I climbed in the backseat and it took us less than five minutes to get to the restaurant. The janitor—I hadn't even bothered to get his name—was already sitting at a table, drinking a cup of coffee.

"So, you say you're a reporter," he asked after I slid into the seat across from him.

I nodded. No sense in speaking a lie any more than I had to.

He took a slow sip of his coffee. "Well, I have some info you may be interested in, but it's gonna cost you."

I braced myself for the worst. I didn't know how much I was willing to pay. But if he came with some ridiculous amount, I was just going to have to cut my losses.

He sat nervously twisting his hands. "It's some good information."

"Okay."

"Some really good information," he repeated.

"I said okay. How much?"

He took a deep breath, then rushed out the words. "A thousand dollars."

I almost fell out of my chair. A thousand dollars? That's all? I had that in my purse. But I knew not to show my hand, so I hesitated, then said, "All right, but this better be good."

His eyes lit up and he said, "It is. It is."

I reached in my purse and he got even more excited.

"I'm going to get the money now?" he asked.

"Yep, if I get the info now."

He all but salivated as I counted out ten one-hundred-dollar bills and slid them across the table.

He snatched the money up and tucked it in the pocket of his hideous plaid shirt. "Get your pen and paper because, boy oh boy, have I got a story for you."

Chapter 40

As the wheels touched down at Miami International Airport, I was still trying to process everything that I'd just learned.

And, boy, had I learned a lot. The question now was what I was going to do with the information that janitor (he never would give me his name) had given me.

I knew that celebrities lied about their age all the time, but Nelly Fulton had taken things to a whole different level. I couldn't wait to look her in her face when I called her on it.

I was just making plans in my head on how I was going to confront her at school tomorrow when I got a tweet that said Join Rumor Central host at the Miami Beach Extravaganza tonight at nine.

I rolled my eyes because I was supposed to be headlining that and they'd just moved Nelly right on in.

"Well, there will be no time like the present," I said, grabbing my purse and making my way out of the plane.

I thought the Miami Beach Extravaganza would be the perfect place to put Nelly Fulton on blast. I checked in with my parents since I'd been gone all day, then I made my way to South Beach, where the event was being held.

I sat toward the back in my shades and a baseball hat that I'd picked up from a vendor. The Miami Beach Extravaganza was a couture swimsuit fashion show, and Nelly was supposed to be the star attraction.

On my way from the airport, I sent out a text to a couple of friends in the media to make sure that they would be there. I wanted everybody to get this.

Finally, about ten minutes after nine, a man walked on to the stage. "Ladies and gentlemen," he said to the now crowded tented area. "I hope you guys are ready! We have a great show for you tonight, and to kick things off and to keep it flowing is *the* diva, the teen queen, the new host of *Rumor Central* and *X Factor* winner . . . Nelly Fulton!"

The crowd started clapping—okay, who am I kidding, they went wild, but I was sure it didn't have anything to do with her hosting *Rumor Central*. It was because of the whole *X Factor* thing. Regardless, I sat there and tried to keep my attitude in check as Nelly walked onto the stage.

"What's up, Miami?" she said, waving to the crowd. "It's your girl Nelly Fulton and I am so happy to be here today! Are y'all ready to have a good time?"

The crowd started screaming. It took everything in my power not to play my hand right there and shut this show down, but I wanted to wait until after the show when the media was in full force. I didn't see the crew from *Miami Hot Gossip* and I definitely wanted to make sure they were front and center. So I sat and I actually enjoyed the fashion show. Nelly did an okay job, but she didn't have the personality that I did. And she was phony as all get out. But I let her do her as I sat and waited for the question-and-answer segment. I actually smiled when I looked back over my shoulder and saw all of the media finally there.

And as soon as the host said, "Okay, before we go, what would the Miami Beach Extravaganza be without hearing from you guys? There are two small mics in the center of the room," he said, pointing to the two mics on the stand. "Come on up if you have a question about the fashions you saw tonight, or if you have a question for our star about her music, her show, or how it feels to be the reigning teen queen. Step right up."

Several people came up and I slowly made my way up behind them, making sure to keep my head down. I waited as four or five people asked frivolous questions about the fashions.

A couple of people asked about her upcoming album and then it was my turn and I slowly stepped to the mic. I eased my sunglasses off, took my hat off, and shook my hair out.

"Oh my God, it's Maya Morgan," someone next to me whispered.

"Hi, Nelly," I said. She looked kind of shocked, but then quickly put the smile back on her face.

"Well, if it isn't the *former* host of *Rumor Central.* Everyone give it up for Maya Morgan!" she said and the crowd actually went wild again. Several people clapped and waved in my direction.

I smiled and leaned in to the mic. "Oh, today isn't about me."

"Well, we know that," she said, cutting me off.

Oh, this was gonna be good. I was going to take great pride in what I was about to say.

"Today is all about you making your debut at the Miami Beach Extravaganza," I continued. "And one of the questions that I have is . . ." I paused as the crowd grew silent. ". . . who is Nadra Franklin?"

The smile completely left Nelly's face, and if it was possible for her to lose all color, she did. Her reaction was enough to send the media scurrying.

"E-excuse me," she stammered.

"Nadra Franklin. You know her, right?" I said a little louder.

She glared at me as the crowd stared at her. "Um, I think that's all of the time we have for questions," she said, turning to the host, who looked confused as well.

"No," I said, speaking loudly into the mic. "I think you should tell these people that *you're* Nadra Franklin."

She glared at me some more. And I smiled.

"And? Your point would be?" she asked, trying to play it cool. But I could tell, she was completely shaken. "People change their names all the time."

"Do people change their ages, too?" I said. I raised my voice as the crowd started chattering. "Ladies and gentlemen, I don't take away from Nadra—I'm sorry, from Nelly—that she's a fantastic singer, but she's also a fraud." I turned to the crowd and pointed to the stage. "Miami, I present to you teen queen, *thirty-one*-year-old Nadra Franklin!"

The crowd went crazy. The photographers started flashing their bulbs. Nelly looked at me like she wanted to kill me. And I turned around and walked out of the room.

I could hear her suddenly begin screaming after me. But I walked out with a smile on my face, ignoring the cameras that were pointed at me and the people who were pulling at me, trying to get more answers. My work was done. I'd put the nugget out there. I had no doubt in my mind these people would get to work and take it from there.

That janitor had been all too happy to sell the story about the small-town girl who had decided to seize her chance at stardom by pretending to be more than ten years younger. He said he'd remained quiet all these years because he didn't want to out his daughter. But since she'd blown off his attempts to rebuild their relationship, he'd decided to make a little money off the story.

I didn't know if he actually was her father. I didn't even really care. He'd given me enough proof that she wasn't who she claimed to be, and that was all I needed. I was sure that the media would dig a whole slew of bones out of Nadra Franklin's closet.

That janitor just didn't know. That was the best thousand dollars I'd ever spent.

Chapter 41

When my mom called me into the kitchen to sit and talk, I just knew she was about to light into me about what had gone down last night. She hated for me to get "down in the gutter" and preferred that I take the high road. But I had to get her to see there was no high road with Nelly Fulton.

"So, you're all over the news today," my mom said.

"I know," I said. "And I know you probably don't approve of what I did."

"Well, I've learned that you have a lot more spunk than your mom. You get that from your father." She patted my hand. "So I'm sure you had your reasons."

"I did," I said, grateful that I wasn't getting a tongue lashing. "I just couldn't let her win."

My mom nodded her understanding. "You know I will still always prefer the high road, but I understand sometimes you have to meet people where they are. And I also know revenge is best served cold."

"What does that mean?" I asked.

"It means that in order to successfully complete an act of revenge, one must be without emotions when carrying out those plans. Emotions will make you lose focus on what you are trying to accomplish, and possibly ruin the act itself. You took your time and thought about this, right? And still decided it was something you needed to do?"

I nodded. "I did. I didn't just react without thinking."

"Then, you did what you had to do." She smiled and we talked for another thirty minutes. It was a rare, intimate conversation. Sometimes my mom got on my nerves, but I did enjoy when we just sat and talked about everything under the sun.

We'd been talking about Alvin and she was giving me advice, relaying the story of her first love and how she'd thought that she'd never get over him.

I was about to ask her a question when my phone rang. I'd been ignoring calls all day, but this one was from Black Tie Productions, the company doing the movie.

"Mom, hold on. I have to get this," I said, pushing the TALK button. "Hello, this is Maya."

"Hi, Maya. This is Robin Teague, assistant production director."

"How are you?"

"I'm well, thanks. Excited about this project. I'm not going to hold you. I just wanted to let you know that I'm going to courier over the final script. We're actually set to film in Miami in three weeks, so I'll need you to get right on your lines. We think you and J. Love are going to be fantastic."

At the mention of J. Love's name, I groaned. Did I really want to work with him after all that we had been through? Since I wasn't ready to quit the movie, I said, "Okay, that's great. I'll get right on it."

After I hung up and explained the situation to my mother, she said, "I am so proud of you. And yes, you can work with J. Love. Do your job and ignore him the rest of the time."

I smiled. She was right. I'd exacted enough revenge. I was just going to do me.

We talked some more, and then my dad walked in, setting his briefcase on the counter.

"How are my two favorite ladies?" He kissed my mom on the lips, then kissed me on the top of the forehead.

"We are great," my mother said. "But guess what? Your daughter is about to officially be a movie star now."

"I thought she was already a star." He winked in my direction.

"*Movie* star," my mother replied. "She got the role in the new Hype Lee film. And they start filming it right after graduation."

"I didn't know she was up for a role in the new Hype Lee film. Nobody tells me anything around here." He playfully pouted. "And since I'm the primary investor in that film, you'd think I'd know these things."

That made me and my mom do a double take. "What do you mean, primary investor?" I asked.

My dad loosened his tie. "You remember I told you I acquired that production company, Black Tie Productions?" he said to my mom. "I have a majority holding."

"What?" I said. "Why didn't you tell me?"

"Yes, why didn't you tell us?" my mom echoed.

"Um, because neither of you ever have any interest in my business. You just want to spend the money my businesses make." He removed his tie and set it across his briefcase.

"And that sounds like it's going to be pretty lucrative," my mom said with a sly smile.

"Remember, you're on a budget," my dad replied, pointing a playful warning finger at my mom.

"Budget, smudget," my mom said, waving him off. She didn't pay him any attention when he complained about money. For her, a budget meant that she could only shop in Paris once a month, instead of twice.

"Okay, Dad, for real. What does that mean, since you're the investor?" My mind was churning.

"It means I pay for everything," my dad said, looking at me like he couldn't figure out why I was quizzing him. He was right, I'd never shown one iota of interest in his business. But that was before he got in the movie business.

"I'll be paying your salary," my dad continued. "So that means you work for me."

"Oh, I need a raise then." I giggled. But then, it dawned on me. Maybe I wasn't through getting my revenge after all. The perfect payback. "I do have a question, Dad. As the majority holder, you really call the shots, right?"

"Yeah, pretty much. But that's why you hire competent people. I try to step back and let them do what they do."

I stood and eased over to him. "Daddyyyyy," I said in my little girl voice. "I do need you to do something."

"What?" He gave me a side eye.

"Well, you know I would never ask something like this, but it's pretty important."

"Oh, spit it out. What is it?"

Even my mom was looking at me funny, trying to figure out what I was up to.

"J. Love is supposed to be the star of that movie. I play his girlfriend."

"Okay?"

"I don't want him in the movie."

"What?"

It was time for me to put my acting chops to work. "Daddy, J. Love hurt me really bad. He broke me and Alvin up, then he was just so mean to me." And, for good measure, I threw in, "And the last time I was over there, I thought he was going to hit me."

"Hit you?" my dad exclaimed. His whole body tensed up like he was about to go into attack mode.

I made sure I cleared that up before my dad was out the door. "But he didn't! I was just worried that he would because he has such an awful temper. That's why I broke up with him, because he's just an awful person and well, I really want this role, but I just don't feel safe with him." I lowered my head, like I was really sad. "I was just telling Mom that I didn't want to take the role because I didn't want to work with him."

"Oh, no!" my dad exclaimed. "Nobody messes with my baby."

"I really don't want to work with him." I dabbed at my eyes, even though there weren't any tears there (guess I still had some work to do on my acting).

"Well, if I had known you were even interested in acting, I would've told you, but now that I know that this is something you want, and you're serious about it, right?"

I nodded. "Yes, I just don't want to do it with J. Love."

"Then I'll make a call. If they want my money, they'll get rid of J. Love."

"I mean, I don't want to mess with your business," I added for good measure.

"You know I usually don't mix business with personal affairs. But I also don't play when it comes to my princess." He stroked my hair. "You don't worry about it. I'll take care of everything."

"Are you sure you can do that?" I asked.

"The man with the money calls the shots. Consider it done."

I gave him an innocent smile as I hugged him. "Thank you, Daddy."

"Of course, sweet pea," he said. "I'm going to make that call right now."

I watched him walk out of the kitchen, and then I turned around to see my mother staring at me as she shook her head. "And the Academy Award goes to my daughter, Maya Morgan," she said.

I braced myself for her to fuss at me, but instead she smiled and said, "I raised you well."

Chapter 42

I told these people I wasn't the one to mess with. But I guess they had to see it for themselves. I wrapped that revenge up in a nice little bow and served it on a silver platter. I leaned back on the sofa and smiled as I watched the TV.

Nelly, or rather Nadra, was scrambling to run from the paparazzi, as they'd been hounding her ever since the story broke. She'd released a statement saying that she was going to rehab to "deal with personal demons" relating to the way she'd been raised. But other than that, she hadn't addressed the issue. But that hadn't stopped the media from hounding her.

"Nelly, why did you do it?" one of the reporters called out after her.

I laughed as she raced to get inside the car.

"Well, as you can see," the *Inside Edition* anchor said, "Nelly Fulton, aka Nadra Franklin, had nothing to say to our cameras. But those that used to know her in the small town of Chattahoochee, Florida, had plenty to say. Our reporter Alisa Moore is there with the story."

The camera switched to the high school I had visited.

Two women were standing next to the reporter as she began talking.

"Good afternoon," the reporter began. "Since she won *X Factor*, we've all thought Nelly Fulton was an orphan from New York, but we're slowly learning that was all part of a story carefully crafted by an ambitious woman who decided to carve out her second chance." The reporter turned to two women standing next to her. Both of them looked like they had lived a hard life. They both had long stringy blond hair, brown, rotting teeth, and wrinkled skin, and one looked like she was one biscuit away from exploding.

"I'm here with Rebecca and Sally. Ladies, tell us again how you knew Nelly?" the reporter asked.

"Nadra—we didn't know Nelly," the first girl said. The name on the screen identified her as Rebecca. "But we all went to school together here in Chattahoochee."

"And I understand you have a yearbook," the reporter said, pointing to the book in the girl's hand.

"Yep." She held up the yearbook and turned it around to face the camera. "Chattahoochee Middle School, 1995," the girl said, doing a Vanna White move as she pointed to the book. She then opened it up. "Nadra Franklin," she said, pointing to a picture of a redheaded girl with oversized glasses and two big front teeth, looking like Peter Rabbit.

"That's Nadra right there," Sally said, tapping the photo. "Before her nose job. She always has been uppity. Poor as dirt but always tried to act like she was better than everybody else."

"So, did you all know that Nelly Fulton was actually Nadra Franklin?" the reporter asked.

"No," Rebecca said.

Sally triumphantly leaned in. "I did. When she was on *X Factor*, I tried to tell everybody that she looked just like Nadra, and everybody thought I was crazy."

"But everything we read said that Nelly was eighteen at the time," Rebecca said. "We all knew that that couldn't be right, so we didn't think it was the same person. I mean, really, who would lie over something like that?"

That was the million-dollar question I had asked myself. It's not like *X Factor* even has an age limit like *American Idol*. So there was no need for Nadra to lie. Guess she'd figured America would have much more sympathy for a young orphan girl.

"Why do you think she lied?" the reporter asked.

"She always has been a liar," Sally added. "When she was in third grade, she said her real parents were Hollywood stars. She said her meth-head mama adopted her."

"What happened to her parents?" the reporter asked.

"Her mother died when we were sophomores in high school and don't nobody know who her daddy is," Rebecca said.

I know, I thought to myself. The janitor told me he'd been a married father of two when he'd gotten Nelly's mother, a local drug addict, pregnant. He'd never claimed Nelly and, in fact, had moved his family away to escape the gossip. He'd said he'd only moved back to Chattahoochee about five years ago.

"Nadra moved to go live with relatives and that's the last we heard of her," Sally added.

Whatever her reasoning, Nelly had really screwed herself up by doing this. I'd read yesterday that *X Factor* was thinking about taking her title away and giving it to the first runner-up, claiming Nelly was guilty of fraud.

"Well, there you have it," the reporter said, turning my attention back to the TV. "Old friends of Nelly Fulton—"

"Nadra," Sally corrected.

"Nadra," the reporter said. "Of course, we'll stay on top of this story and bring you more as we get it. Back to you."

I could only shake my head. I didn't know where Nadra

would end up, but maybe she would think twice before she screwed over the next person.

I flipped through the TV and started looking for something else to watch when the buzzer rang, letting me know somebody was at the gate. I glanced at the security system, and rolled my eyes when I saw Tamara of all people. I started not to buzz her in, but I had been waiting on this day. I needed to see her face-to-face, if for no other reason than to gloat.

I walked over to meet Tamara at the front door. I didn't know why she was here. The lawsuit had been thrown out, but I supposed she was coming here to apologize. At least, she *needed* to be coming here to apologize.

I watched her pull her silver Bentley into our circular driveway and then strut up the walkway like the true diva that she was. But I was no longer impressed with Tamara. She'd proven to be as ruthless as they come, and I had almost followed in her footsteps. I was glad that I hadn't.

"Hey, Maya," she said as she approached the doorway.

"Hey," was all I replied. I wasn't going to be nasty, but I wasn't going to fake the funk either.

"Can I come in?" Tamara asked.

I didn't say a word as I stepped aside and motioned for her to come in.

She looked around our grand foyer. "I always have loved the color scheme in here," she said, taking in the copper-colored walls. "Your mother has such exquisite taste."

"I'm sure you didn't come over here to talk décor," I told her as I closed the front door. "So how can I help you?"

She turned to face me, moving her Hermès bag to her other arm. "Look, let me just get straight to the point."

"That's always best," I replied.

She took a deep breath, then said, "I'm sorry. You were right. We shouldn't have tried to bring Nelly on board."

I just raised an eyebrow, but didn't say a word.

"I'm sure you can imagine this has been a disaster for *Rumor Central* and the execs are having a stroke. We're about to go into the summer blockbuster season. MTV has that new show coming that is supposed to rival *Rumor Central,* and now is just not the time for us to be trying to start over."

I gave her an *And I care because?* look, but still kept quiet.

"So I'm just here to say I'm sorry."

"Okay," was all I replied.

"And um, we were wondering . . ." She paused and took a deep breath. "We were hoping that you'd consider returning to *Rumor Central.*"

I couldn't help it. That actually made a smile come back on my face, and that seemed to make her relax some.

"I mean, I know you were upset about the way everything went down, and we'd be willing to give you a significant pay raise—"

"You know this was never about the money with me," I was quick to tell her.

"I know that, but we want to show you how sorry we are and to make this right. Yes, *Rumor Central* has some issues, but we believe in the show, the public still likes the show, and I think if we sit down and put our heads together we can figure out a way to make this thing right."

I actually laughed at that. "You know, I enjoyed my time at *Rumor Central,*" I told her. "It really brought me to the next level. I'll give you guys that, but it was me and my hard work and connections that made the show. And somewhere along the way, you seem to have forgotten that."

"Okay, you're right." Tamara sighed. "What can I say? Just come back and we'll fix it."

I looked as if I was weighing what she was saying, and then finally I said, "You know what? I'm flattered. I really am. I'd like nothing more than to return to *Rumor Central.*"

A look of relief crossed her face, and I quickly held up my hand before she could say anything.

"But I think it's best that we continue our separate ways."

"Excuse me?" She had the nerve to look dumbfounded, like she'd never expected me to say no. She must not have known me at all.

I walked back over to the door. "Tamara, I have no desire to return to *Rumor Central,* or to you and your backstabbing team of producers, so good luck finding a replacement. Good luck cleaning up the mess that Nelly—I'm sorry—that Nadra Franklin made, and please leave my house."

She didn't move as she said, "I heard about you in the new Hype Lee movie. You really want to bank on that?"

"Yeah. I'm branching out to acting, and guess what? If it doesn't work out, I'm cool with that. In case you haven't realized"—I looked around at my massive home—"I'll be well taken care of regardless, so I'll be on to bigger and better things."

"Maya, you're being unreasonable. I get that you're mad. If it's more power you want, we can work with that. If you want us to put it in writing that we won't bring on a cohost without your consent, we can put that in writing, too. Just, please, come back to *Rumor Central.*"

I opened the front door and smirked at her, before saying, "Tamara, don't beg, it's not a good look."

She stepped on the other side of the door, and turned around and snarled at me.

"I hope you know what you're doing."

I just looked at her and said, "I do."

Then, I took great pride as I slammed the door in her face.

Chapter 43

My day was finally here, and I didn't think it could get any more perfect.

"You look beautiful," my mother said, adjusting my cap.

I never thought I'd be so happy to be walking across a stage. But I was actually about to get my high school diploma and, on Monday, begin filming my first movie.

Rumor Central had been the springboard to launch me into the national spotlight, and I was about to take it from here.

"So, are you ladies ready?" my dad asked. I was thrilled that he had cleared his entire schedule for the weekend. While for some families that may be no biggie, for my dad it was huge. Even my mom was shocked.

"We're so beyond ready," Sheridan said.

Sheridan and Kennedi stood next to me in the small private dressing area. I don't know how my dad had done it, but he'd gotten me a private room at the arena where our graduation was being held so that I could have an intimate reception before the graduation.

Kennedi actually had to take one more class this summer because not all of her credits had transferred. But luckily, her father had pulled some strings and gotten her permission to walk with us. I would've been sick if I hadn't been able to walk across that stage with my two best friends.

"Come on, honey. Let's go to our seats," my mom said to my dad. She kissed me on the cheek. "We'll see you out there," she added before leading my dad out.

"I'm going to meet you guys out there," Sheridan told me. "My mom wants me to come say hello to her new man." She shook her head. But I knew Sheridan was glad that her mother, Ms. Glenda, had taken a pause from her world tour to be here today because even though she never admitted it, I think there was a part of Sheridan that was worried her mom would miss her graduation altogether.

"Okay, see you in a minute."

She hadn't been gone two minutes when J. Love pushed his way into the room.

"What did you do?" he screamed at me.

It caught me off guard, but I didn't flinch. I hadn't heard from him since I'd stormed out of his place. My dad had told me that the producers had agreed to take him off the movie, but I hadn't heard anything since. But I guess J. had finally gotten the word.

"Hello, J. Love," I said with a smile. "I don't recall your name being on my private reception guest list."

"Maya, don't play with me. My agent called and told me that I'm not doing the movie." He looked frazzled, not his usual cool self.

"Really? And we start filming next week," I innocently said. "Oh, well. I'll tell you all about it."

"You wouldn't be in this movie if it wasn't for me."

"Then I'll have to send you a thank-you card from the set," I told him.

He stepped closer. I guess he was trying to intimidate me. But it didn't work. "Maya, what did you do?"

"I am flattered that you think I have that much power.

And maybe I do. Or maybe I don't." I turned to the mirror and checked my reflection, completely dismissing him. "But isn't karma a b—"

He cut me off. "How did you do it?"

I turned back to face him. "Do what?"

He studied me for a minute, then said, "Nah, you ain't got that much juice."

"Okay." I could just see his mind churning as he tried to figure it out.

"Come on, K. We should go," I said to Kennedi.

J. Love jumped in front of me to stop me from passing. "If I find out you had anything to do with this . . ."

". . . you're not going to do a thing."

I turned toward the door and my heart fluttered at the sight of Alvin standing in the entrance.

"Alvin!" I said, pushing past J., and rushing over to throw my arms around Alvin's neck.

"Hey, pretty lady," he said, hugging me tightly.

"I can't believe you came."

"Now, you know I wasn't going to miss this day," he replied.

"Look, bruh. Me and Maya are talking," J. said.

Alvin eased me behind him. "Nah, bruh. You and Maya are done."

"Dude, you have no idea who you're talking to."

"No, you have no idea." Alvin stepped in his face. "Don't let the bowtie fool you."

J. Love looked a little surprised. He wasn't the only one. This was a side of Alvin I hadn't seen.

They had a face-off, and then J. licked his lips and smiled. "You know, you need to be thanking me."

I cringed because I figured he was about to throw in Alvin's face how he got the job.

But Alvin shocked us all, when he said, "You know, I do. Because you've made me a very rich man."

The smile left J.'s face and Alvin continued.

"Yeah, see they explained to me how I got hired. And of course, when I found that out, I said thanks, but no thanks. I don't need any hookups from the likes of you."

"You quit?" I said, my heart racing at the thought that he could be moving back home.

"Yeah," he finally turned to me and smiled, "but not before Microsoft bought my new patent."

"Oh my God," I squealed. "Are you serious?"

"Yep. Seven figures, baby." He turned, picked me up and swung me around. After he set me down, he turned back to J. Love. "So yeah, I guess I should be thanking you for putting me on their radar because you made me a very rich man."

J. Love looked horrified, but he pulled himself together. "Whatever. Maya, I'm not done talking to you."

"Yeah, you are." Alvin patted J. Love's chest. "I know you play hard. And I know you think I'm soft, but I promise you don't want none of this." He adjusted J.'s collar. "I mean, it would be real bad for your image to get beat down by a nerd boy, don't you think?"

J. Love looked like he was weighing his options. Finally, he said, "Man, ain't nobody scared of you."

Alvin grinned. "You don't have to be. The bottom line is you and I can settle our beefs at another time. Today is Maya's day."

I couldn't help but smile.

"Since I saw you coming in, I thought we might need these gentlemen. Security here is gonna escort you out." He pointed to two men who appeared in the doorway.

"Is he bothering you, ma'am?" the first officer said.

"Yes, he sure is," I replied.

"Oh, it's like that, Maya?" J. Love snapped.

I draped my arm through Alvin's. "It is. Bye-bye."

"Oh, this isn't over. Nobody plays J. Love."

"It looks like somebody just did." Kennedi chuckled.

"Get your hands off of me," he said, jerking his arm away from the security guard who was trying to lead him out.

"We'd better get going," Kennedi said, looking out the door. "They're starting to line up."

"Okay, you go on," I told her. "I'll be right out. I just want to talk to Alvin real quick."

Kennedi smiled. "Good to see you, Superman."

He returned her smile. "You, too, K."

Once we were alone, I knew I didn't have much time to waste. "I'm sorry about everything," I said.

"It's cool," he said.

"So, you're really moving back home?" I asked.

He nodded. "I am."

"So, what does that mean for us?"

His smile left his face, but not his eyes. "It means I miss my friend and that's where I want to go back to. Just being friends."

I'm not going to lie, that hurt my heart. But if I couldn't have him as my boyfriend, I'd settle for him as my friend. And as he'd once told me, I would just have to work to win him back.

"Come on, let's go get this diploma," he told me. "You know how hard you had to work to get here."

"You ain't never lied." I laughed.

"Hey, how are things with *Rumor Central*?" he asked as we headed to the door.

"Now that they've discovered Nelly is a thirty-one-year-old poser, it didn't go over well. They wanted me back, but I said no. I heard they're planning on canceling the show."

"How do you feel about that?" he asked.

"I'm good. I left on top."

He hugged me tightly. "And when it comes to Maya Morgan, I wouldn't expect anything else."

EYE CANDY

ReShonda Tate Billingsley

ABOUT THIS GUIDE

The following questions are intended to
enhance your group's reading of
EYE CANDY.

DISCUSSION QUESTIONS

1. Initially, Maya really wanted to make her relationship with Alvin work. Why do you think she kept getting sucked into doing things with J. Love?

2. J. Love was relentless in his pursuit of Maya. Why do you think he wanted her so bad? Do you think his feelings for her were genuine?

3. Maya kept saying that what she was doing with J. Love was just for show. Do you think she was wrong for that, or should Alvin have been more understanding?

4. Nelly shocked everyone when her secret was exposed. Why do you think she lied? Do you think she would've had the same success if she had been truthful?

5. Tamara and the *Rumor Central* producers didn't seem to have any loyalty to anyone. Do you think they grew tired of Maya, or was it really all about the ratings?

6. Maya was quick to believe Marisol when she said she was moving with Alvin. Why do you think she didn't give Alvin the benefit of the doubt?

7. Do you think Alvin put up with a lot from Maya? Why do you think he finally snapped?

8. Was Maya wrong to expose Nelly the way she did? Why do you think she did it?

9. Maya used her father to pull J. Love from the movie. Do you think she should've done that? Or did J. Love deserve it?

10. Alvin ended up on top, by selling his patent to Microsoft. Since he'd moved back to Miami, do you think Alvin should've given Maya another chance?

Meet Maya for the first time in

Rumor Central

The teen reality show *Miami Divas* made media sensations out of Miami's richest in-crowd—and Maya Morgan is one of them. Now Maya's been offered her very own show, and she'll do whatever it takes to step up the fame she's worked so hard for—and that includes spilling some secrets her friends wish were left buried. But as Maya gives up the goods for the sake of ratings, someone will do anything to shut her up. Between backstabbing lies and hard truths, this gossip girl has only one chance to make things right . . . before it's too late.

Available wherever books and ebooks are sold.

Turn the page for an excerpt from *Rumor Central* . . .

Chapter 1

"*A*in't *no party like a Maya Morgan party, 'cuz a Maya Morgan party don't stop!*"

The sounds of the screeching crowd filled The Mansion, Miami's hottest club. Usually reserved for the twenty-one and up crowd, tonight it was closed down just for me!

That's because I got it like that. Just ask any one of the fifteen-hundred people crowded into The Mansion to celebrate my birthday.

Forget Sweet Sixteen, my Sweet *Seventeen* party was one for the history books. MTV was here filming, my reality show *Miami Divas* was taping our season finale, and the dee-jay had the crowd on their feet, leading them with the chant that everyone was singing.

"*Ain't no party like a Maya Morgan party, cuz a Maya Morgan party don't stop!*"

If I wasn't on top of the world before, I was definitely on it now.

I stood in the VIP box overlooking the dance floor, waving my hands back and forth with the music. My swag was in full force. I was rocking an emerald green Valentino lace tank dress, some five-inch gold Giuseppe Zanotti peep toe pumps and enough jewelry to feed a small village in China. I'd gotten highlights in my jet black, long wavy hair and of course, my makeup was on point.

That's how I roll. My mom says I'm "extra" but I say I'm about that life, that's why when MTV contacted me last year about being on their show "My Super Sweet Sixteen," I told them I was an extraordinary type of girl and I didn't want to do any ordinary type of show. So, I was going to wait a year and do a Sweet *Seventeen* party.

They weren't feeling me at first, but the way the cameraman was panning the hyped up crowd, and the producer was grinning from ear to ear, I knew they were feeling me now.

"Girl, this party is hot!" my friend, Kennedi, said as she bounced to the music. She was rocking a Versace royal blue jumpsuit and looked almost as tight as me. Almost.

"And you thought it wouldn't be?" I laughed as I took another sip of my drink. "You know how I do it."

She laughed, then looked around. "Where's your little crew at?"

I knew it was just a matter of time. Kennedi and I have been friends since we were babies because our mothers had been college roommates. But she lived in Orlando now, so we didn't get to hang as much. For some reason, she didn't cut for my new friends, especially the ones from my reality show *Miami Divas*.

The show starred me and four of my classmates from our private school, Miami High. Don't get it twisted; we weren't your ordinary high school students. If you looked up fab in the dictionary, it would have our picture right next to it. Shoot, Kimora Lee Simmons named her company—Fabulosity—directly after me. (Well, that's my story anyway.) But when you had more money in your purse than most people made in a year, you had no choice but to be fab. And me and my crew were all that and a bag of jalapeño chips.

There was my BFF, Sheridan Matthews. Her mom is world-renowned singer Glenda Matthews. Then, Shay Turner, who can best be described as my frenemy because she's so ghetto-fabulous (and I don't do ghetto) that we clash like oil and water. But her dad, Jalen Turner, is like the biggest basketball player in the country, so she was rolling in dough. The other crew members included Evian Javid, who had more money than all of us combined because her dad is this Middle Eastern billionaire; Bali Fernandez, who I just adore because he is so over-the-top and doesn't care who knows it—including his uptight daddy who is some kind of Cuban diplomat. And then me—you ever heard of the Morgan Hotel chain? That's right, I'm *that* Morgan. Don't hate. Although if you did, I'd be used to it. I'm a five-foot-nine, caramel coated princess. When you put us all together, you had fabulousity at its finest.

I don't know if Kennedi just didn't like the crew or if she was jealous that Sheridan had taken her spot (that's what she always said). So she didn't like the others, but she *despised* Sheridan. And the feeling was mutual.

"They're in the back doing some interviews," I finally said, answering her.

She turned up her nose. "This is about you. Why are they doing interviews?"

I smiled. "Chill, Kennedi. It's all good. My party is going to be part of the season finale."

"I thought this was supposed to just be for MTV."

"They worked out something." I shrugged. I left all those kinds of details to my dad and our attorney.

She finally laughed. "Only you would be able to get MTV to change their whole programming lineup."

"Hey, hey, hey!" my girl Lauren sang as she approached us. Even though the club was dark, I could tell by the way she was slurring her words that she was high as a kite. Back in the day, me, Kennedi and Lauren were inseparable. But her parents had shipped her off to boarding school and she'd turned into a druggie. Since I don't do druggies, we'd drifted apart.

Still, I knew she'd be too through if I didn't invite her to the party, so I'd let her come, but I'd told her to leave all that drug mess alone. Obviously, she didn't listen.

"What's up, girl?" I said, shaking my head at her. She was too pretty to be messing herself up like that. She looked like a younger version of Jada Pinkett Smith and could've been a model or an actress. But now, she stayed too high to do much of anything. "Glad you could make it."

"Sorry I was late. I was ummm, ah . . ." She started giggling.

"Yeah, we know what you were doing," Kennedi snapped. We'd both tried talking to Lauren, but any progress we made with her was lost when she went back to school.

I turned my attention back to the crowd that was now jamming to a TI song. Lauren wasn't about to put a damper on my party.

"Where's your boo?" Lauren asked, looking around the VIP section, which held only about twenty people: my executive producer from *Miami Divas*, Tamara Collins, who also happened to be an old family friend; some MTV executives; my other friends from school, Chenoa, Chastity, and Ava; and a couple of my other close friends.

I smiled as my eyes made their way across the crowded dance floor to my baby, my first love, Bryce Logan. The definition of fine, Bryce had it going on—from his hazel brown eyes to his curly brown hair—he looked like he could be Chris Brown's younger (and much cuter) brother. Bryce's dad played for the Miami Dolphins, and it was his dream to do the same and he was definitely on his way as the star running back at Miami High.

"My boo is over there talking to his friends. I can't wait to see what he got me for my birthday."

"Probably a new BMW," Kennedi joked.

"All I want to know is how can I find me a baller's son?" Lauren said.

"Try saying crack is whack and you might be able to," Kennedi replied.

Lauren looked insulted. "I don't do crack."

"Oh, sorry." Kennedi shrugged and rolled her eyes. "Ecstasy, dope?"

I finally decided to step in. "Hey, you two don't start. This is all about me today."

Kennedi laughed and bumped me, almost making me spill my drink. "Girl, when is it *not* all about you?"

Before I could answer, Sheridan bounced into the VIP area. "Hey, Maya," she said. "Come on, the producers are waiting on you."

Kennedi cut her eyes. "Is Maya the only one you see?"

Sheridan stopped, looked at her, looked around, then turned to Kennedi and said, "Yep." She took my hand and tried to lead me off. "Come on, girl."

I could see Kennedi about to get worked up.

"Chill," I mumbled. The last thing I wanted was any drama at my party. "I'll be right back. Go get a drink. You know my mom is watching the punch like a hawk but I think Carl and his crew have some of the good stuff in the back." I could tell the way Kennedi's nostrils were flaring that she wanted to say something else. But she let it slide.

"Good stuff? I'm coming with you," Lauren threw in.

"I don't know how you can keep being friends with them," Sheridan said as we headed to the back.

I stopped to face her. "Okay, I'm going to tell you like I told them. Today is all about me. I'm not trying to do the drama, ya feel me?"

"Fine, fine, fine," Sheridan said as she draped her arm through mine and giggled. "Girl, this party is sooo tight!"

I was glad she let it drop as we walked into the back room where they were shooting some scenes from the season finale of *Miami Divas*. The show had done well in our first year on the air. We'd been one of the TV station's highest rated shows.

"If it isn't the fabulous Maya Morgan," Bali said as I walked over to where he and the others stood in a small circle waiting on direction from the producer. Bali was the flamboyant one of the group and today was no exception. He was Versace'd down—from the silk shirt to the skinny jeans. And his Louboutins were badder than mine.

"You know I'm sick over the shoes," I told him as we air-kissed.

He stuck his foot out and wiggled it. "Eat your heart out, honey. One of a kind." He leaned in closer. "But, missy, I need to talk to you about your guest list."

"What are you talking about?"

"Ummm, yeah, the two Pillsbury Dough girls that have been following me around the party."

I laughed. I knew exactly who he was talking about. "You mean Nina and Tina."

"Nina and Tina, Bina and Kina, whatever. Their names need to be Krispy and Kreme because they look like some fluffy glazed donuts."

"Boy, stop." I laughed.

"Unh-unh. Just a hot mess." He shook his head in disgust.

"Believe me, if I could've left them off, I would have. But they're my cousins."

"Ugh, don't tell anyone else that," Evian added.

"Yeah, you need to get your fam off the buffet table," Shay threw in.

I laughed. Leave it to my crew. You couldn't even tell just 24 hours ago, we were arguing like crazy because they didn't like the idea of filming the season finale at my party because as Shay said, "This show ain't about *her*." But as we always did, we'd worked through our differences. That's because we were a team, in this thing together. And I wouldn't have it any other way!